RACING
in the RAIN

MY LIFE AS A DOG

GARTH STEIN

RACING in the RAIN

MY LIFE AS A DOG

HARPER

An Imprint of HarperCollinsPublishers

Library of Congress Cataloging-in-Publication Data is available.
ISBN 978-0-06-293507-6 (pbk.)

Typography by Sasha Illingworth
19 20 21 22 23   PC/BRR   10 9 8 7 6 5 4 3 2 1
❖
First special edition, 2019

For Muggs

"With your mind power,
your determination,
your instinct,
and the experience as well,
you can fly very high."
—AYRTON SENNA

one

Gestures are all that I have; sometimes they must be grand in nature. And while I occasionally cross the line into the world of the melodramatic, it is what I must do in order to communicate clearly and effectively. In order to make my point understood. I have no words I can rely on because, much to my dismay, my tongue was designed long and flat and loose. It is a horribly ineffective tool for pushing food around my mouth while chewing. And an even less effective tool for making clever and complicated sounds that can be linked together to form sentences. And that's why I'm here now waiting for Denny to come home. He should be here soon. I'm lying on the cool tiles of the kitchen floor in a puddle of my own urine.

I'm old. And while I'm very capable of getting older,

that's not the way I want to go out. Shot full of pain medication to reduce the swelling of my joints. Vision fogged with cataracts. Puffy, plasticky packages of Doggie Depends stocked in the pantry. I'm sure Denny would get me one of those little wagons I've seen on the streets, the ones that cradle the hindquarters so a dog can drag his butt behind him when things start to fail. That's humiliating and degrading. I'm not sure if it's worse than dressing up a dog for Halloween, but it's close. He would do it out of love, of course. I'm sure he would keep me alive as long as he possibly could. But I don't want to be kept alive. Because I know what's next. I've seen it on TV. A documentary I saw about Mongolia. It was the best thing I've ever seen on television, other than the 1993 Grand Prix of Europe, of course. That was the greatest automobile race of all time, in which Ayrton Senna proved himself to be a genius in the rain. After the 1993 Grand Prix, the best thing I've ever seen on TV is a documentary that explained everything to me, made it all clear. It told the whole truth: when a dog is finished living his lifetimes as a dog, his next life will be as a man.

I've always felt almost human. I've always known that there's something about me that's different than other dogs. Sure, I'm stuffed into a dog's body, but that's just the shell. It's what's inside that's important. The soul. And my soul is very human.

The door opens, and I hear him with his familiar cry, "Yo, Zo!" Usually, I can't help but put aside my pain and hoist myself to my feet. Then I'll wag my tail, sling my tongue around, and shove my face into his crotch. It takes humanlike willpower to hold back on this particular occasion, but I do. I hold back. I don't get up. I'm acting.

"Enzo?"

I hear his footsteps, the concern in his voice. He finds me and looks down. I lift my head, wag my tail feebly so it taps against the floor. I play the part.

He shakes his head and runs his hand through his hair. He sets down the plastic bag from the grocery that has his dinner in it. I can smell roast chicken through the plastic. Tonight he's having roast chicken and an iceberg lettuce salad.

"Oh, Enz," he says.

He reaches down to me, crouches, touches my head like he does, along the crease behind the ear. Then I lift my head and lick at his forearm.

"What happened, kid?" he asks.

Gestures can't explain.

"Can you get up?"

I try, and I scramble. My heart takes off, lunges ahead

because no, I can't. I panic. I thought I was just acting, but I really can't get up. Darn. Life imitating art.

"Take it easy, kid," he says, pressing down on my chest to calm me. "I've got you."

He lifts me easily, he cradles me, and I can smell the day on him. I can smell everything he's done. His work, the auto shop where he stands behind the counter all day. He makes nice with the customers who yell at him because their BMWs don't work right and it costs too much to fix them. And that makes them mad so they have to yell at someone. I can smell his lunch. He went to the Indian buffet he likes. All you can eat. It's cheap, and sometimes he takes a container with him and steals extra portions of the tandoori chicken and yellow rice and has it for dinner, too. I can smell beer. He stopped somewhere. The Mexican restaurant up the hill. I can smell the tortilla chips on his breath. Now it makes sense. Usually, I'm excellent at keeping track of time, but I wasn't paying attention because of my emotional thoughts.

He places me gently in the tub and turns on the handheld shower thing and says, "Easy, Enz."

He says, "Sorry I was late. I should have come straight home, but the guys from work insisted. I told Craig I was quitting, and . . ."

I didn't want him to feel bad about this. I wanted him

to see the obvious. That it's okay for him to let me go. He's been going through so much, and he's finally through it. He needs to not have me around to worry about anymore. He needs me to free him to be brilliant.

He is so brilliant. He shines. He's beautiful with his hands that grab things and his tongue that says things. And the way he stands and chews his food for so long, mashing it into a paste before he swallows. I will miss him and little Zoë, and I know they will miss me. But I can't let these feelings get in the way of my grand plan. After this happens, Denny will be free to live his life, and I will return to earth in a new form, as a man. And when I return I will find him and shake his hand and comment on how talented he is. Then I will wink at him and say, "Enzo says hello," and turn and walk quickly away. "Do I know you?" he will call, "Have we met before?"

After the bath he cleans the kitchen floor while I watch. He gives me my food, which I eat too quickly again, and sets me up in front of the TV while he prepares his dinner.

"How about a tape?" he says.

"Yes, a tape," I reply, but of course, he doesn't hear me.

He puts in a video from one of his races and he turns it on and we watch. It's one of my favorites. The racetrack is dry for the pace lap. Then, just after the green flag is waved, indicating the start of the race, there is a wall of rain, a torrential downpour that engulfs the track. All the cars around him spin out of control, and he drives through them as if the rain didn't fall on him. It's like he had a magic spell that cleared water from his path. Just like the 1993 Grand Prix of Europe, when Senna passed four cars on the opening lap. And these were four of the best championship drivers in their championship cars— Schumacher, Wendlinger, Hill, Prost. He passed them all like he had a magic spell.

Denny is as good as Ayrton Senna. But no one sees him because he has responsibilities. He has his daughter, Zoë, and he had his wife, Eve, who was sick until she died, and he has me. And he lives in Seattle when he should live somewhere else. And he has a job. But sometimes when he goes away he comes back with a trophy. He shows it to me and tells me all about his races and how he shone on the track. How he'd taught those other drivers in Sonoma or Texas or Mid-Ohio what driving in wet weather is really about.

When the tape is over, he says, "Let's go out," and I struggle to get up.

He lifts my butt into the air and centers my weight over my legs, and then I'm okay. To show him, I rub my muzzle against his thigh.

"There's my Enzo."

We leave our apartment; the night is sharp, cool, and breezy and clear. We only go down the block and back because my hips hurt so much, and Denny sees. Denny knows. When we get back, he gives me my bedtime cookies and I curl into my bed on the floor next to his. He picks up the phone and dials.

"Mike," he says. Mike is Denny's friend from the shop where they both work behind the counter. Customer relations, they call it. Mike's a little guy with friendly hands that are pink and always washed clean of smell. "Mike, can you cover for me tomorrow? I have to take Enzo to the vet again."

We've been going to the vet a lot recently to get different medicines that are supposed to help make me more comfortable. But they don't, really. And since they don't, and considering all that went on yesterday, I've set the Master Plan in motion.

Denny stops talking for a minute, and when he starts again, his voice doesn't sound like his voice. It's rough, like when he has a cold or allergies.

"I don't know," he says. "I'm not sure it's a round trip visit."

I may not be able to form words, but I understand them. And I'm surprised by what he said, even though I set it up. For a moment, I'm surprised my plan is working.

It *is* the best thing for all involved, I know. It's the right thing for Denny to do. He's done so much for me, my whole life. I owe him the gift of setting him free. Letting him rise up. We had a good run, and now it's over; what's wrong with that?

two

He picked me out of a pile of puppies, a tangled, rolling mass of paws and ears and tails. We were behind a barn in a smelly field near a town in eastern Washington called Spangle. I don't remember much about where I came from, but I remember my mother. She was a big Labrador who would walk slowly across the yard as my littermates and I chased after her. Honestly, our mother didn't seem to like us much, and she was fairly indifferent to whether we ate or starved. She seemed relieved whenever one of us left. One fewer yipping puppy tracking her down to drain her of her milk.

I never knew my father. The people on the farm told Denny that he was a shepherd-poodle mix, but I don't believe it. I never saw a dog that looked like that on the farm. The lady was nice, but the alpha man—the guy in charge—was mean. He would look you in the eyes and lie even if telling the truth was just as easy. He went on at length about the differences in intelligence of dog breeds. He firmly believed that shepherds and poodles were the smart ones but that Labradors were more gentle. Therefore a puppy would be more desirable—and more valuable—if it was a mix of these breeds. All a bunch of junk. Everyone knows that shepherds and poodles aren't especially smart. They're responders and reactors, not independent thinkers. Especially the blue-eyed sheepdogs from Down Under—Australia—that people make such a fuss over when they catch a Frisbee. Sure, they're clever and quick, but they don't think outside the box; they're all about convention.

I'm sure my father was a terrier. Because terriers are problem solvers. They'll do what you tell them, but only if it happens to be in line with what they wanted to do anyway. There was a terrier like that on the farm. An Airedale. Big and brown-black and tough. No one messed with him. He didn't stay with us in the gated field behind the house. He stayed in the barn down the hill by the creek, where the men went to fix their tractors. But sometimes he would come up the hill, and when he did, everyone steered clear. Word in the field was he was a fighting dog the alpha man kept separate because he'd kill a dog for sniffing in his direction. He'd rip the fur from a dog's neck because of a lazy glance. And when a female dog was in heat, he'd mate with her and go about his business without a thought about who was watching or who cared. I've often wondered if he's in fact my father. I have his brown-black coloring and my coat is slightly wiry, and people frequently comment that I must be part terrier. I like to think I am.

I remember the heat on the day I left the farm. Every day was hot in Spangle, and I thought the world was just a hot place because I never knew what cold was about. I had never seen rain, didn't know much about water. Water was the stuff in the buckets that the older dogs drank, and it was the stuff the alpha man sprayed out of the hose and into the faces of dogs who might want to pick a fight. But the day Denny arrived was exceptionally hot. My littermates and I were tussling around like we always did, and a hand reached into the pile and suddenly I was dangling high in the air.

"This one," a man said.

It was my first glimpse of the rest of my life. He was slender, with long and lean muscles. Not a large man, but strong. He had keen, icy blue eyes. His choppy hair and short, scruffy beard were dark and wiry, like an Irish terrier.

"The pick of the litter," the lady said. She was nice; I always liked it when she cuddled us in her soft lap. "The sweetest. The best."

"We were thinkin' a keepin' 'im," the alpha man said, stepping up with his big boots caked with mud from the creek, where he was patching a fence. That was the line he always used. Heck, I was a pup only a dozen weeks old, and I'd already heard that line a bunch of times. He used it to get more money.

"Will you let him go?"

"Fur a price," the alpha man said, squinting at the sky, bleached a pale blue by the sun. "Fur a price."

three

"Very gently. Like there are eggshells on your pedals," Denny always says, "and you don't want to break them. *That's* how you drive in the rain."

When we watch videos together—which we've done ever since the very first day I met him—he explains these things to me. (To me!) Balance, anticipation, patience. These are all vital. Using your side vision, seeing things you've never seen before. Feeling the road, driving by the seat of the pants. But what I've always liked best is when he talks about having no memory. No memory of things he'd done just a second before. Good or bad. Because memory is time folding back on itself. To remember is to leave the present. In order to reach any kind of success in automobile racing, a driver must never remember.

This is why drivers compulsively record their every

move, their every race, with cockpit cameras and in-car video. A driver cannot be a witness to his own greatness. This is what Denny says. He says racing is doing. It is being a part of a moment in time and being aware of nothing else but that moment. The great champion Julian SabellaRosa has said, "When I am racing, my mind and my body are working so quickly and so well together, I must be sure not to think, or else I will definitely make a mistake."

four

Denny moved me far from the farm in Spangle to a Seattle neighborhood called Leschi. He lived in a little apartment he rented on Lake Washington. I didn't enjoy apartment living much, as I was used to wide-open spaces. And I was very much a puppy. Still, we had a balcony that overlooked the lake, which gave me pleasure since I am part water dog, on my mother's side.

I grew quickly, and during that first year, Denny and I forged a deep fondness for each other as well as a feeling of trust. Which is why I was surprised when he fell in love with Eve so quickly.

He brought her home and she was sweet smelling, like him. Full of fermented drinks that made them both act funny, they were hanging on each other and pulling at each other, tugging, and biting playfully. It kind of reminded me of the way I used to wrestle with my litter-mates. Only different somehow.

When he went to the bathroom, she patted my head, which hovered low to the floor. Me still being immature at just over a year old, and a little bit intimidated by all the goings-on. She said, "You don't mind if I love him, too, do you? I won't come between you."

I respected her for asking, but I knew that she *would* come between us, and I found her denial to be untruthful.

I tried not to act off-putting because I knew how much Denny liked her. But I have to admit that I didn't embrace her presence. And because of that, she was less than embracing of me. We were both satellites orbiting Denny's sun, struggling for his affection. Of course, she had the advantage of her tongue and her thumbs, and when I watched her kiss and hold his hand sometimes she would glance at me and wink as if to gloat: *Look at my thumbs! See what they can do!*

five

Monkeys have thumbs.

Practically the dumbest species on the planet, but monkeys have thumbs. Those monkey thumbs were meant for dogs. Give me my thumbs, you darned monkeys!

I watch too much TV. When Denny goes away in the mornings, he turns it on for me, and it's become a habit. He warned me not to watch all day, but I do. Fortunately, he knows I love cars, so he lets me watch a lot of Speed Channel. The classic races are the best, and I especially like Formula One.

Sometimes if I'm watching the History Channel or the Discovery Channel I learn about other cultures and other ways of life. Then I start thinking about my own place in the world and what makes sense and what doesn't.

The scientists go on and on about how monkeys are

the closest evolutionary relative of people. But that's spec-
ulation. Based on what? Based on the fact that certain
ancient skulls have been found to be similar to modern
man's? What does that prove? So what if man's body
evolved from the monkeys? Whether he came from monkeys or fish is unimportant. The important idea is that
when the body became "human" enough, the first human
soul slipped into it.

I'll give you a theory: Man's closest relative is not
the chimpanzee, as the TV people believe, but is, in fact,
the dog.

Case-in-Point: The Werewolf

The full moon rises. The fog clings to the lowest
branches of the spruce trees. The man steps out of the
darkest corner of the forest and finds himself transformed
into . . .

A *monkey?*

I think not.

Six

Her name was Eve, and at first I resented how she changed our lives. I resented the attention Denny paid to her small hands and her slender body. The way he gazed into her soft green eyes, which peered out from under stylish strands of straight blond hair. Did I envy her engaging smile? Perhaps I did. For she was a person, unlike me. She was well groomed. Unlike me. She was everything I wasn't. I went for extended periods without a haircut or a bath, for instance; she bathed every day and had a special person do nothing else but color her hair. My nails grew too long and scratched the wood floor; she frequently attended to her nails with sticks and clippers and polishes to make sure they were the proper shape and size.

Her attention to every detail of her appearance was

reflected in her personality as well. She was an incredible organizer, constantly making lists and jotting down notes of things to be done. Our weekends were filled with trips to the Home Depot or waiting in line at the Disposal and Recycling Station in Georgetown. I didn't like painting rooms and fixing doorknobs and washing screens. But Denny liked it, apparently, because the more she gave him to do, the more quickly he completed his tasks. Then he collected his reward, which usually included a lot of nuzzling and kissing.

Soon after she moved into our apartment, they were married in a small wedding ceremony. I attended along with a group of their closest friends and Eve's immediate family. Denny didn't have any brothers or sisters to invite, and he explained his parents' absence simply by saying that they didn't travel well.

The wedding took place at a charming little beach cottage on Whidbey Island. Eve's parents made it clear to all involved that the house was owned by close friends of theirs. I was allowed to participate only under strict rules. I was not to roam freely on the beach, as I might track sand onto the expensive mahogany floors. And I was forced to do my "business" in a very specific location next to the recycling containers.

Upon our return from Whidbey, I noticed that Eve

moved through our apartment with a greater sense of ownership. She was much bolder in her actions to move or replace things: towels, linens, and even furniture. She had entered our lives and changed everything around. And yet, while I was unhappy with her intrusion, there was something about her that prevented me from being really angry with her. I believe that thing was her swollen belly.

True, I was very jealous of the attention Eve lavished on her unborn baby. But, looking back, I realize I had never given her a reason to give that same attention to me. Perhaps that is my regret. I loved how she was when she was pregnant, and yet I knew I could never be the source of her affection in that way because I could never be her child.

She devoted herself to the baby before it was even born. She touched it regularly through her tightly stretched skin. She sang to it and danced with it to music she played on the stereo. She learned to make it move around by drinking orange juice, which she did frequently. She once asked if I wanted to know what it felt like, and I did, so she held my face against her belly after she had drunk the juice, and I felt it move. It was hard for me to imagine exactly what was going on behind the magic curtain. But I knew that what was inside of her was separate from her, and had a will of its own.

I admire the female sex. The life makers. It must be amazing to have a body that can carry an entire creature inside. (I mean, other than a tapeworm, which I've had. That doesn't count, really.) The life that Eve had inside her was something she had made. She and Denny had made it together. I wished, at the time, that the baby would look like me.

I remember the day the baby arrived. I had just reached adulthood—two years by calendar count. Denny was in Daytona, Florida, for the drive of his career. He had spent the entire year contacting sponsors, begging, pleading, and hustling. One day he got lucky and found the right person in the right hotel lobby to say, "You've got guts, son. Call me tomorrow." Thus, he found his long-sought sponsor dollars and was able to buy a seat in a Porsche 993 for the twenty-four-hour race at Daytona.

Endurance racing is not for the meek. Four drivers each spending six hours behind the wheel of a loud, powerful race car is an exercise in determination. The 24 Hours of Daytona is as unpredictable as it is exciting. That Denny was presented with a chance to drive it in the same year that his daughter would be born was one of those coincidences that was open to interpretation. Eve was dismayed by the unfortunate timing of the events; Denny celebrated the great opportunity and the feeling that he had everything he could possibly ask for.

Still, the timing was off. On the day of the race, Eve felt the contractions and called the midwives. They came and invaded our home and quickly took charge. Later that evening, as Denny was driving at Daytona, Eve stood bent over the bed with two round ladies who helped her by holding her arms. Then, with a monstrous bellow that seemed to last an hour, out squirted a little wet blob that wriggled spastically and then cried out. The ladies helped Eve into her bed and rested the tiny purple thing on her chest until the baby's searching mouth found Eve's breast and began to feed.

"Could I have a minute alone—?" Eve started.

"Of course," one of the ladies said, moving to the door.

"Come with us, puppy," the other lady said to me on her way out.

"No"—Eve stopped them—"He can stay."

I could stay? Despite myself, I felt proud to be included in Eve's inner circle. The two ladies bustled off, and I watched in fascination as Eve suckled her new babe. After a few minutes, my attention drifted from the baby's first meal to Eve's face, and I saw that she was crying and I wondered why.

She let her free hand dangle to the bedside, her fingers near my muzzle. I hesitated. I didn't want to presume she was beckoning me. But then her fingers wiggled and her eyes caught mine, and I knew she was calling me. I bumped her hand with my nose. She lifted her fingers to the crown of my head and scratched, still crying, her baby still nursing.

"I know I told him to go," she said to me, referring to Denny. "I know that I insisted he go, I know." Tears ran down her cheeks. "But I *so* wish he were here!"

I had no idea what to do, but I knew not to move. She needed me there.

"Will you promise to always protect her?" she asked.

She wasn't asking me. She was asking Denny, and I was merely Denny's substitute. Still, I felt the obligation. I understood that, as a dog, I could never be as connected as I truly desired. Yet, I realized at that moment, I could be something else. I could provide something of need to the people around me. I could comfort Eve when Denny was away. I could protect Eve's baby. And while I would always want more, in a sense, I had found a place to begin.

The next day, Denny came home from Daytona, Florida, unhappy. His mood immediately changed when he held his little girl, whom they named Zoë, not after me, but after Eve's grandmother. "Do you see my little angel, Enz?" he asked me.

Did I see her? I practically *birthed* her!

Denny was very careful around Eve's parents. Maxwell and Trish had been in the house since Zoë was born, taking care of their daughter and their new baby granddaughter. I began calling them the Twins because they looked very much alike. They had the same shade of dyed hair. Plus they always wore matching outfits: khaki pants or polyester slacks with sweaters or polo shirts. When one of them wore sunglasses, the other did, too. The same with Bermuda shorts and tall socks pulled up to their knees. And because they both smelled of chemicals: plastics and hair products.

From the moment they arrived, the Twins had been criticizing Eve for having her baby at home. They told her she was endangering her baby's welfare. And that in these modern times, it was irresponsible to give birth anywhere but in the best of all hospitals with the most expensive of all doctors. Eve tried to explain to them that statistics showed exactly the opposite was true for a healthy mother. Also, that any signs of distress would have been recognized early by her experienced team of midwives. But the Twins didn't understand. Fortunately for Eve, Denny's arrival home meant the Twins could turn their attention away from her faults and focus on his.

As they stood in the kitchen, Denny told Maxwell about the disappointing results of the race at Daytona.

"That's a lot of bad luck," the male Twin said to Denny as they stood in the kitchen. Maxwell was gloating; I could hear it in his voice.

"Do you get any of your money back?" Trish asked.

Denny was very unhappy, and I wasn't sure why until Mike came over later that night and he and Denny opened their beers together. It turned out that Denny had been going to take the third stint driving at Daytona. The car had been running well, everything going great. They were in second place and Denny would easily take the lead as the sunlight faded and the night driving began. Until the guy who had the second turn driving slammed the car into the wall on turn 6.

He crashed it when a Daytona Prototype—a much faster car—was overtaking. First rule of racing: Never move aside to let someone pass; make *him* pass *you*. But the driver on Denny's team moved over, and he hit a bad patch on the track. When he did, the rear end snapped around and he plowed into the wall at pretty close to top speed. The car shattered into a million little pieces.

The driver was unhurt, but the race was over for the team. And Denny, who had spent a year working for this moment, found himself standing by the side of the racetrack watching the opportunity of his lifetime get dragged away by a tow truck. He hadn't had a chance to sit in it for a single racing lap.

"And you don't get any of your money back," Mike said, after Denny had finished telling his story.

"I don't care about any of that," Denny said. "I should have been here."

"The baby came early. You can't know what's going to happen before it happens."

"Yes, I can," Denny said. "If I'm any good, I can."

"Anyway," Mike said, lifting his beer bottle, "to Zoë."

"To Zoë," Denny echoed.

To Zoë, I said to myself. *Whom I will always protect.*

seven

When it was just Denny and me, he used to make up to ten thousand dollars a month in his spare time by selling things to people over the telephone. But after Eve became pregnant, Denny took his job behind the counter at the fancy auto shop. The one that serviced only expensive German cars. Denny liked his job, but it ate up all of his free time, and he and I didn't get to spend our days together anymore.

Sometimes on weekends, Denny taught at a high-performance drivers' school run by one of the many car clubs in the area—BMW, Porsche, Alfa Romeo. He often took me to the track with him. I enjoyed these outings very much. He didn't really like teaching at these events because he didn't get to drive; he just had to sit in the passenger seat and tell other people how to drive.

He fantasized about moving somewhere—to Sonoma or Phoenix, or even Europe—and catching on with one of the big schools so he could drive more. Eve said she didn't think she could ever leave Seattle.

Eve worked for some big clothing company because it provided us with money and health insurance. Also because she could buy clothes for the family at the employee discount. She went back to work a few months after Zoë was born, even though she really wanted to stay home with her baby.

With Denny and Eve working and Zoë off at day care, I was left to my own devices. For most of the dreary days I was alone in the apartment, wandering from room to room, from nap spot to nap spot. I spent a lot of time doing nothing more than staring out the window. I hadn't realized how much I enjoyed having everyone bustling around the house for those first few months of Zoë's life. I had felt so much a part of something. I played a role in Zoë's entertainment.

Sometimes after a feeding, when she was awake and alert and strapped safely into her bouncy seat, Eve and Denny would play Monkey in the Middle. They would throw a ball of socks back and forth across the living room; I got to be the monkey. I leapt after the socks and then scrambled back to catch them. Then I danced like a four-legged clown to catch them again. And when I reached the sock ball and batted it into the air with my snout, Zoë would squeal and laugh; she would shake her legs with such force that the bouncy chair would scoot along the floor. And Eve, Denny, and I would collapse in a pile of laughter.

But then everyone moved on and left me behind.

I sank into the emptiness of my lonely days. I would stare out the window and try to picture what it was like before everyone went away, how much fun we all had together. But it didn't help much. Until one day when a fortunate accident happened that changed my life. Denny turned on the TV in the morning to check the weather report, and he forgot to turn the TV off.

Let me tell you this: The Weather Channel is not about weather; it is about the *world*! It is about how weather affects us all, our entire global economy. Also our health, happiness, and spirit. The channel goes into great detail about weather of all different kinds—hurricanes, tornadoes, hail, rain, lightning storms. Absolutely fascinating. So much so that when Denny returned from work that evening, I was still glued to the television.

"What are you watching?" he asked when he came in, as if I were Eve or Zoë. As if it couldn't have been more natural to see me there or address me like that. But Eve was in the kitchen cooking dinner and Zoë was with her; it was just me. I looked at him and then back to the TV, which was showing the day's major event: flooding due to heavy rainstorms on the East Coast.

"The Weather Channel?" he scoffed, snatching up the remote and changing the channel. "Here."

He changed it to Speed Channel.

I had watched plenty of TV as I grew up, but only when a person was already watching: Denny and I enjoyed racing and the movie channels. Eve and I watched music videos and Hollywood gossip. Zoë and I watched children's shows. (I tried to teach myself to read by studying *Sesame Street*, but it didn't work.) Suddenly, the idea of watching television by *myself* entered my life! If I had been a cartoon, the lightbulb over my head would have lit up. I barked excitedly when I saw cars racing on the screen. Denny laughed.

"Better, right?"

Yes! Better! I stretched deeply, joyously, doing my best downward-facing dog and wagging my tail—both gestures of happiness and approval. And Denny got it.

"I didn't know you were a television dog," he said. "I can leave it on for you during the day, if you want."

I want! I want!

"But you have to limit yourself," he said. "I don't want

to catch you watching TV all day long. I'm counting on you to be responsible."

I am responsible!

I had learned a great deal up until that point in my life. But once Denny began leaving the TV on for me, my education really took off. With the boredom gone, time started moving quickly again. The weekends, when we were all together, seemed short and filled with activity. And while Sunday nights were bittersweet, I took great comfort in knowing I had a week of television ahead.

I was so immersed in my education, I suppose I lost count of the weeks. So I was surprised by the arrival of Zoë's second birthday. Suddenly I was engulfed by a party in the apartment with a bunch of little kids. It was loud and crazy, and all the children let me play with them and wrestle on the rug. I even let them dress me up with a hat and a sweat jacket, and Zoë called me her big brother. They got lemon cake all over the floor, and I got to be Eve's helper cleaning it up while Denny opened presents with the kids. She used a Dustbuster and I used my tongue.

After everyone had left and we had all completed our cleaning assignments, Denny had a surprise birthday present for Zoë. He showed her a photograph that she looked at with little interest. But then he showed the same photograph to Eve, and it made Eve cry. And then it made her laugh and she hugged him and looked at the photo again and cried some more. Denny picked up the photograph and showed it to me, and it was a photo of a house Denny had bought.

"Look at this, Enzo," he said. "This is your new yard. Aren't you excited?"

I guess I was excited. Actually, I was kind of confused. I didn't understand the implications. And then everyone started shoving things into boxes and scrambling around, and the next thing I knew, my bed was somewhere else entirely.

The house was nice. It was a stylish little bungalow like I'd seen on *This Old House*, with two bedrooms and only one bathroom but with plenty of living space. It was situated very close to its neighbors on a hillside in the Central District.

Eve and Denny were in love with the place. They spent almost the entire first night there strolling around in every room except Zoë's. When Denny came home from work, he would first say hello to the girls, then he would take me outside to the yard and throw the ball, which I happily retrieved. And then Zoë got big enough that she would run around and squeal while I pretended to chase her.

And Eve would admonish her: "Don't run like that; Enzo will bite you."

She did that frequently in the early years, doubt me like that. But one time, Denny turned on her quickly and said, "Enzo would never hurt her—ever!" And he was right. I knew I was different from other dogs. I had a certain willpower that was strong enough to overcome my instincts. What Eve said was not out of line. Most dogs cannot help themselves; if they see an animal running, they go after it. But that sort of thing doesn't apply to me.

Still, Eve didn't know that, and I had no way of explaining it to her, so I never played rough with Zoë. I didn't want Eve to start worrying. Because I had already smelled it. When Denny was away and Eve fed me and she leaned down to give me my bowl of food and my nose was near her head, I had detected a bad odor, like rotting wood, mushrooms, decay. Wet, soggy decay. It came from her ears and her sinuses. There was something inside Eve's head that didn't belong.

Given a speaking tongue, I could have told them. I could have alerted them to her condition long before they discovered it with their machines, the computers and supervision scopes that they use to see inside the human head. They may think those machines are sophisticated, but in fact they are clunky and clumsy. My nose—yes, my little black nose that is leathery and cute—could smell the disease in Eve's brain long before even she knew it was there.

But I couldn't talk. So all I could do was watch and feel empty inside; Eve had assigned me to protect Zoë no matter what, but no one had been assigned to protect Eve. And there was nothing I could do to help her.

eight

One summer Saturday afternoon, we spent the morning at the beach at Alki swimming and eating fish and chips from Spud's. When we returned to the house, red and tired from the sun, Eve put Zoë down for a nap; Denny and I sat in front of the TV to study.

He put on a tape of a long-distance race he had driven in Portland a few weeks earlier. It was an exciting race, eight hours long, in which Denny and his two co-drivers took turns behind the wheel in two-hour shifts. They came in first after Denny's last-minute heroics, which included recovering from a near spin to overtake two competitors.

Denny started the tape at the beginning of his final stint. The track was wet and the sky heavy with dark clouds that threatened more rain. We watched several laps in silence. Denny drove smoothly and almost alone. His team had fallen behind after making the crucial decision to pull into the pits and switch to rain tires; other racing teams had predicted the rain would pass and so had gained more than two laps on Denny's team. Yet the rain began again, which gave Denny a great advantage.

Denny quickly and easily passed cars from other classes. There were underpowered Miatas that darted through the turns with their excellent balance; big-engine Vipers with their lousy handling. Denny, in his quick and muscular Porsche, slicing through the rain.

"How come you go through the turns so much faster than the other cars?" Eve asked.

I looked up. She stood in the doorway, watching with us. "Most of them aren't running rain tires," Denny said.

Eve took a seat on the sofa next to Denny. "But some of them are."

"Yes, some," he said. We watched. Denny drove up behind a yellow Camaro at the end of the back straight. And though it looked as if he could have taken the other car in turn 12, he held back. Eve noticed.

"Why didn't you pass him?" she asked.

"I know him. He's got too much power and would just pass me back on the straight. I think I take him in the next series of turns." Yes. At the next turn, Denny was inches from the Camaro's rear bumper. He rode tight through the double turn and then took the inside line for the next turn and he zipped right by.

"This part of the track is really slick in the rain," he said. "He has to back way off. By the time he gets his grip back, I'm out of his reach."

On the back straight again, the Camaro could be seen in Denny's rearview mirror, fading into the background.

"Did he have rain tires?" Eve asked.

"I think so. But his car wasn't set up right."

"Still. You're driving like the track isn't wet, and every-one else is driving like it is."

Turn 12 and blasting down the straight, we could see brake lights of the competition flicker ahead; Denny's next victims.

"We are the creators of our own destiny," Denny said softly.

"What?" Eve asked.

"When I was nineteen," Denny said after a moment, "at my first driving school down at Sears Point, it was raining and they were trying to teach us how to drive in the rain. After the instructors were finished explaining all their secrets, all the students were totally confused. We had no idea what they were talking about. I looked over at the guy next to me—I remember him, he was from France and he was very fast. He smiled and he said, 'We are the creators of our own destiny.'"

Eve stuck out her lower lip and squinted at Denny. "And then everything made sense," she said jokingly.

"That's right," Denny said seriously.

On the TV, the rain didn't stop; it kept coming. Denny's team had made the right choice; other teams were pulling off into the hot pits to change to rain tires.

"Drivers are afraid of the rain," Denny told us. "Rain makes your mistakes even worse, and water on the track can make your car handle unpredictably. When something unpredictable happens, you have to react to it; if you're reacting at speed, you're reacting too late. And so you *should* be afraid."

"I'm afraid just watching it," Eve said.

"If I intentionally make the car do something, then I can predict what it's going to do. In other words, it's only unpredictable if I'm not . . . *possessing* . . . it."

"So you spin the car before the car spins itself?" she asked.

"That's it! If I deliberately do something, then I know it's going to happen before it happens. Then I can react to it before even the car knows it's happening."

"And you can do that?"

On the TV screen, Denny could be seen dashing past other cars. His rear end suddenly slipped out and his car

got sideways. But his hands were already turning to correct, and he was off again, leaving the others behind. Eve
sighed in relief, held her hand to her forehead.

"I love you," she said. "I love all of you, even your
racing. And I know on some level that you are completely
right about all this. I just don't think I could ever do it
myself."

She went off into the kitchen; Denny and I continued
watching the cars on the video as they drove around and
around the circuit drenched in darkness.

I will never tire of watching tapes with Denny. He
knows so much, and I have learned so much from him.
He said nothing more to me; he continued watching his
tapes. But my thoughts turned to what he had just taught
me. Such a simple concept, yet so true: we are the creators
of our own destiny. Be it through intention or ignorance,
our successes and our failures have been brought on by
none other than ourselves.

I left Denny at the TV and walked into the kitchen.
Eve was preparing dinner, and she looked at me when I
entered.

"Bored with the race?" she asked casually.

I wasn't bored. I could have watched the race all that
day and all the next. I was creating my own destiny. I lay

down near the refrigerator, in a favorite spot of mine, and rested.

I could tell she felt self-conscious with me there. Usually, if Denny was in the house, I spent my time by his side; that I had chosen to be with her now seemed to confuse her. She didn't understand my intentions. But then she got rolling with dinner, and she forgot about me.

First she started some hamburger frying, which smelled good. Then she washed some lettuce and spun it dry. She sliced apples. She added onions and garlic to a pot and then a can of tomatoes. And the kitchen was rich with the smell of food. The smell of it and the heat of the day made me feel quite drowsy, so I must have nodded off. Then I felt her hands on me, stroking my side, then scratching my belly, and I rolled over on my back to acknowledge her; my reward was more of her comforting scratches.

"Sweet dog," she said to me. "Sweet dog."

She returned to her preparations, pausing only occasionally to rub my neck with her bare foot as she passed, which wasn't all that much, but meant a lot to me anyway. I reached out to Eve, and she responded—a connection was made. Denny was right: We *are* the creators of our own destiny.

nine

A couple of years after we moved into the new house, something very frightening happened.

Earlier that spring Denny had gone to France for a Formula Renault testing program. He did exceptionally well in this program because it was in France in the spring, when it rains. When he told Eve about it, he said that one of the scouts who attend these things approached after the session and said, "Can you drive as fast on dry tracks as you can on wet ones?" And Denny looked him straight in the eyes and replied, simply, "Try me."

The scout offered Denny a tryout, and Denny went away for two weeks. Testing and tuning and practicing. It was a big deal. He did so well, they offered him a seat in the endurance race at Watkins Glen.

When he first left for New York, we all grinned at

each other because we couldn't wait to watch the race on Speed Channel. "It's so exciting." Eve would giggle. "Daddy's a professional race car driver!"

And Zoë, whom I love very much and would not hesitate to sacrifice my own life to protect, would cheer and hop into her little race car they kept in the living room. Then she would drive around in circles until we were all dizzy and then throw her hands into the air and proclaim, "I am the champion!"

I got so caught up in the excitement, I was doing idiotic dog things like digging up the lawn. Balling myself up and then stretching out on the floor with my legs straight and my back arched and letting them scratch my belly. And chasing things. I chased!

It was the best of times. Really.

And then it was the worst of times.

Race day came, and Eve woke up very early feeling awful. She had a pain so terrible that she stood in the kitchen and vomited violently into the sink. She vomited as if she were turning herself inside out.

"I don't know what's wrong with me, Enzo," she said. And she rarely spoke to me candidly like that. Like how Denny talks to me, as if I'm his true friend, his soul mate. The last time she had talked to me like that was when Zoë was born.

But this time she did talk to me like I was her soul mate. She asked, "What's wrong with me?"

She knew I couldn't answer. And I felt totally frustrated because *I had an answer.*

I knew what was wrong, but I had no way to tell her. So I pushed at her thigh with my muzzle. I nosed in and buried my face between her legs. And I waited there, afraid.

"I feel like someone's crushing my skull," she said. I couldn't respond. I had no words. There was nothing I could do. "Someone's crushing my skull," she repeated.

And quickly she gathered some things while I watched. She shoved Zoë's clothes in a bag and some of her own and toothbrushes. All so fast. And she roused Zoë and stuffed her little-kid feet into her little-kid sneakers and—*bang*—the door slammed shut. And then—*snick, snick*—the dead bolt was thrown and they were gone.

And I wasn't gone. I was there. I was still there.

ten

Ideally, a driver is a master of all that is around him, Denny says. Ideally, a driver controls the car so completely that he corrects a spin before it happens. He anticipates all possibilities. But we don't live in an ideal world. In our world, surprises sometimes happen, mistakes happen. Incidents with other drivers happen, and a driver must react.

When a driver reacts, Denny says, it's important to remember that a car is only as good as its tires. If the tires lose their grip, nothing else matters. Not engine power, speed, or braking. Nothing else counts when a skid starts. Until the tires regain their grip, the driver is unable to control the car. And that's a bad situation.

It is important for the driver to override his natural fear. When a car begins to spin, the driver may panic and lift his foot off the gas. If he does, he will throw the weight of the car toward the front wheels. Then the rear end will snap around, and the car will spin.

A good driver will try to stop the spin by turning his wheels in the direction the car is moving. He may succeed. However, at a critical point, the skidding stops, and suddenly the tires grip the road but his front wheels are now turned in the wrong direction. This causes a counterspin in the other direction. This secondary spin is much faster and more dangerous.

If, however, when his tires begin to break free, our driver *increases* the pressure on the accelerator, and at the same time eases out on the steering wheel ever so slightly, this will lessen the lateral g-forces at work. The spin will therefore be corrected.

So, our driver is still in control of his car. He is still able to act in a positive manner. He still can create an ending to his story in which he completes the race without incident. And, perhaps, if his creating is good, he will win.

eleven

When I was locked in the house suddenly and firmly, I did not panic. I quickly and carefully took stock of the situation and understood these things: Eve was ill, and the illness was possibly affecting her judgment. Also she likely would not return for me; I knew that Denny would be home on the third day, after two nights.

I am a dog, and I know how to go without food. For three days I took care to ration the toilet water. I wandered around the house sniffing at the crack beneath the pantry door and fantasizing about a big bowl of my kibble. I was able to scoop up the occasional dust-covered Cheerio Zoë had dropped in a corner somewhere. And I did my business on the mat by the back door, next to the laundry machines. I did not panic.

During the second night, approximately forty hours

into my solitude, I think I began to see things that weren't there. I heard a sound coming from Zoë's bedroom. When I investigated, I saw something terrible and frightening. One of her stuffed animal toys was moving about on its own.

It was the zebra. The now-living zebra said nothing to me at all, but when it saw me it began a dance, a twisting, jerky ballet. It began to tease and taunt a Barbie doll. That made me quite angry, and I growled at the evil zebra, but it simply smiled and continued, this time picking on a stuffed frog, which it rode like a horse, its hoof in the air like a bronco rider, yelling out, "Yee-haw! Yee-haw!"

I stalked the zebra as it abused and humiliated each of Zoë's toys. Finally, I could take no more and I moved in, teeth bared for attack, to end the brutality once and for all. But before I could get the crazed zebra in my fangs, it stopped dancing and stood on its hind legs before me. Then it tore at the seam that ran down its belly. Its own seam! It ripped the seam open until it was able to reach in and tear out its own stuffing. It continued to take itself apart, handful by handful, until it was nothing more than a pile of fabric and stuffing.

Shocked by what had happened, I left Zoë's room, hoping that what I had seen was only in my mind. A vision driven by the lack of food. But I knew that it wasn't a vision; it was true. Something terrible had happened.

The following afternoon, Denny returned. I heard the taxi pull up, and I watched him unload his bags and walk them up to the back door. I didn't want to seem too excited to see him. Yet at the same time I was concerned about what I had done to the doormat, so I gave a couple of small barks to alert him. Through the window, I could see the look of surprise on his face. He took out his keys and opened the door, and I tried to block him, but he came in too quickly and the mat made a squishy sound. He looked down and carefully hopped into the room.

"What the heck? What are you doing here?"

He glanced around the kitchen. Nothing was out of place, nothing was amiss, except me.

"Eve?" he called out.

But Eve wasn't there. I didn't know where she was, but she wasn't with me.

"Are they home?" he asked me.

I didn't answer. He picked up the phone and dialed.

"Are Eve and Zoë still at your house?" he asked without saying hello. "Can I speak to Eve?"

After a moment, he said, "Enzo is here."

He said, "I'm trying to understand it myself. You left him here?"

I couldn't hear what was being said on the other end of the line, but I could imagine.

Denny said, "This is insane. How could you not remember that your dog is in the house?"

He said, "He's been here the whole time?"

He said very angrily, "Darn it!"

And then he hung up the phone and shouted in frustration, a big long shout that was very loud.

He walked through the house quickly. I didn't follow him; I waited by the back door. A minute later he returned.

"This is the only place you used?" he asked, pointing at the mat. "Good boy, Enzo. Good work."

He got a garbage bag out of the pantry and scooped the sopping mat into it, tied it closed, and put it on the back porch. He mopped up the area near the door.

"You must be starving." He filled my water bowl and gave me some kibble, which I ate too quickly and didn't enjoy, but at least it filled the empty space in my stomach. In silence, angry, he watched me eat. And very soon, Eve and Zoë arrived on the back porch.

Denny threw open the door.

"Unbelievable," he said bitterly. "You are unbelievable."

"I was sick," Eve said, stepping into the house with Zoë hiding behind her. "I wasn't thinking."

Zoë slipped out from behind her mother and scurried

down the hallway toward her room.

"You should have taken him with you or dropped him at the kennel or something," Denny said.

"I didn't mean to leave him," she whispered.

I heard weeping and looked over. Zoë stood in the door to the hallway, crying. Eve pushed past Denny and went to Zoë, kneeling before her.

"Oh, baby, we're sorry we're fighting. We'll stop. Please don't cry."

"My animals," Zoë whimpered.

"What happened to your animals?" Eve led Zoë by the hand down the hall. Denny followed them. I stayed where I was. I wasn't going near that room where the dancing freak zebra had been. I didn't want to see it.

Suddenly, I heard thundering footsteps. Denny hurtled through the kitchen toward me. He was puffed up and angry and his eyes locked on me. "You stupid dog," he growled.

He dragged me through the kitchen and down the hall, into Zoë's room, where she sat, stunned, on the floor in the middle of a huge mess. Her dolls, her animals, all torn to shreds, a complete disaster. Total ruin. I could only assume that the evil demon zebra had reassembled itself and destroyed the other animals after I had left. I should have eliminated the zebra when I had my chance.

I should have eaten it, even if it had killed me.

Denny was so angry that his anger filled up the entire room, the entire house. Nothing was as large as Denny's anger. "Bad dog!" he bellowed, and he raised his hand.

"Denny, no!" Eve cried. She rushed to me and covered me with her own body. She protected me.

Denny stopped. He wouldn't hit her. No matter what. Just as he wouldn't hit me. He *hadn't* wanted to hit me, I know. He wanted to hit the demon, the evil zebra, the dark creature that possessed the stuffed animal. Denny believed the evil demon was in me, but it wasn't. I saw it. The demon had possessed the zebra and left me at the bloody scene with no voice to defend myself—I had been framed.

"We'll get new animals, baby," Eve said to Zoë. "We'll go to the store tomorrow." As gently as I could, I slunk toward Zoë, the sad little girl on the floor, surrounded by the rubble of her toys, tears on her cheeks. I crawled to her on my elbows and placed my nose next to her thigh. And I raised my eyebrows slightly as if to ask if she could ever forgive me for not protecting her animals.

She waited a long time to give me her answer, but she finally gave it. She placed her hand on my head and let it rest there. She didn't scratch me. It would be a while before she allowed herself to do that. But she did touch me, which meant she forgave me for what had happened.

Later, after everyone had eaten and Zoë was put to bed, I found Denny sitting on the porch steps with a drink of hard liquor, which I thought was strange because he hardly ever drank hard liquor. I approached cautiously, and he noticed.

"It's okay, boy," he said. He patted the step next to him, and I went to him. I sniffed his wrist and took a tentative lick. He smiled and rubbed my neck.

"I'm really sorry," he said. "I lost my mind."

Denny finished his drink with a long swallow and shivered. He produced a bottle from nowhere and poured himself another. He stood up and took a couple of steps and stretched to the sky.

"We got first place, Enzo. We took first place overall. You know what that means?" My heart jumped. I knew what it meant. It meant that he was the champion. It meant he was the best! "It means a seat in a touring car next season, that's what it means," Denny said to me. "I got an offer from a real, live racing team. Do you know what an offer is?

"Getting an offer means I can drive if I come up with my share of sponsorship money for the season. And if I'm willing to spend six months away from Eve and Zoë and you. Am I willing to do that?"

I didn't say anything because I was torn. I knew I was

Denny's biggest fan and supporter of his racing. But I also felt something like what Eve and Zoë must have felt whenever he went away. I got a hollow pit in my stomach at the idea of his absence. He must have been able to read my mind, because he gulped at his glass and said, "I don't think so, either." Which was what I was thinking.

"I'm taking those stuffed animals out of your allowance," he said with a chuckle. He looked at me then, took my chin with his hand.

"I love you, boy," he said. "And I promise I'll never hurt you. No matter what. I'm really sorry."

He was blathering, he was drunk. But it made me feel so much love for him, too.

"You're tough," he said. "You can do three days like that because you're one tough dog."

I felt proud.

"I know you'd never do anything deliberately to hurt Zoë," he said.

I laid my head on his leg and looked up at him.

"Sometimes I think you actually understand me," he said. "It's like there's a person inside there. Like you know everything."

I do, I said to myself. *I do*.

twelve

Eve's condition was unpredictable. One day she would suffer a crushing headache. Another day, a terrible stomachache. A third would open with dizziness and end with a dark and angry mood. And these days were never linked together in a row. Between them would be days or even weeks of life as usual. And then Denny would get a call at work, and he would run to Eve's assistance. He'd drive her home from her job and spend the rest of the day watching helplessly.

Denny felt powerless, and in that regard, I could understand his point of view. It's frustrating for me to be unable to speak. To feel that I have so much to say, so many ways I can help, but I can't.

Denny avoided the madness of his situation by driving through it. There was nothing he could do to make Eve's distress go away, and once he realized that, he made a commitment to do everything else better.

Often things happen to race cars in the heat of the race. A transmission may break, suddenly leaving the driver without all of his gears. Or perhaps a clutch fails. Brakes go soft from overheating. Suspensions break. When faced with one of these problems, the poor driver crashes. The average driver gives up. The great drivers drive through the problem. They figure out a way to continue racing. A true champion can accomplish things that a normal person would think impossible.

Denny cut back his hours at work so he could take Zoë to her preschool. In the evenings after dinner, he read to her and helped her learn her numbers and letters. He took over all the grocery shopping and cooking. He took over the cleaning of the house. He wanted to relieve Eve of any burden, any job that could cause stress. What he couldn't do, though, was continue to engage her in the same affectionate way I had grown used to seeing. It was impossible for him to do everything. Clearly, he had decided that care of her would receive the topmost priority. Which I believe was the correct thing for him to do under the circumstances. Because he had me.

Denny did not stop loving Eve; he merely delegated his love-giving to me. I became the provider of love and comfort. When she ailed and he took charge of Zoë and whisked her out so that she might not hear the cries of agony from her mother, I stayed behind. He trusted me. He would tell me, as he and Zoë packed their bottles of water and cookies, "Go take care of her for me, Enzo, please."

And I did. I took care of her by curling up at her bedside. Or, if she had collapsed on the floor, by curling up next to her there. Often, she would hold me close to her, hold me tight to her body, and when she did, she would tell me things about the pain.

Demon. Gremlin. Ghost. Phantom. Shadow. Devil. People are afraid of them, so they pretend they exist only in stories. In books that can be closed and put on the shelf. They clench their eyes shut so they will see no evil. But trust me when I tell you that devils like the zebra are real. Somewhere, the zebra is dancing.

The spring finally came to us after an exceptionally wet winter. It was full of gray days and rain and an edgy cold I found depressing. Over the winter, Eve ate poorly and became thin and pale. Denny was concerned, but Eve never heeded his pleas for her to consult a doctor. A mild case of depression, she would say. They'll try to give her pills and she doesn't want pills. And one evening after dinner, which was a special one, though I don't remember if it was a birthday or an anniversary, Denny suddenly took Eve into his arms and kissed her.

It seemed so odd to me because they hadn't acted that way with each other in such a long time. But their exchange seemed weak and unenthusiastic. She smiled at him, but she was pretending, I could tell, because she looked at me over Denny's shoulder and waved me off. Respectfully, I withdrew to another room and drifted into a light sleep. And, if I recall correctly, I dreamed of the zebra.

thirteen

Denny had started to act oddly. The clues were all there, I simply hadn't read them correctly. Over the winter, he had played a video racing game obsessively, which wasn't like him. He had never gotten into racing games. But that winter, he played the game every night after Eve went to bed. And he raced on American circuits only. St. Petersburg and Laguna Seca. Road Atlanta and Mid-Ohio. I should have known just from seeing the tracks he was racing. He wasn't playing a video game, he was studying the circuits. He was learning turning points and braking points. I'd heard him talk about how accurate the backgrounds are on these video games. How drivers have found the games can be quite helpful for getting acquainted with new racetracks. But I never thought—

And his diet: no alcohol, no sugar, no fried foods.

His exercise routine: running several days a week, swimming at the Medgar Evers Pool. And lifting weights in the garage of the big guy down the street. Denny had been preparing himself. He was lean and strong and ready to do battle in a race car. And I had missed all the signs. But then, I believe I had been duped. Because when he came downstairs with his track bag packed that day in March and his suitcase on wheels and his special helmet, Eve and Zoë seemed to know all about his leaving. He had told *them*. He hadn't told *me*.

The parting was strange. Zoë was both excited and nervous, Eve was somber, and I was utterly confused. *Where was he going?* I raised my eyebrows, lifted my ears, and cocked my head; I used every facial gesture at my disposal in an attempt to glean information.

"Sebring," he said to me, reading my mind the way he does sometimes. "I took the seat in the touring car, didn't I tell you?"

The touring car? But that was something he said he could never do! We agreed on that! I was at once happy and sad. He would be away so much of the time! I was worried about the emotional well-being of those of us left behind.

But I am a racer at heart, and a racer will never let something that has already happened affect what is happening now. I wagged my tail enthusiastically, and he smiled at me with a twinkle in his eye. He knew that I understood everything he said.

"Be good, now," he said playfully. "Watch over the girls."

He hugged little Zoë and kissed Eve gently, but as he turned away from her she launched herself into his chest and grabbed him tight. She buried herself in his shoulder, her face red with tears.

"Please come back," she said, her words muffled by his mass.

"Of course I will. I promise," he said, hopefully.

After he had gone, Eve closed her eyes and took a deep breath. When she opened her eyes again, she looked at me, and I could see that she had resolved something for herself as well.

"I insisted he do it," she said to me. "I think it will be good for me; it will make me stronger."

That was the first race of the series, and the race didn't go well for Denny, though it went fine for Eve, Zoë, and me. We watched it on TV, and Denny qualified in the top third of the field. But shortly into the race, he had to return to the pit because of a cut tire. Then a crew member had trouble mounting the new wheel, and by the time Denny returned to the race, he was a lap down and never recovered. Twenty-fourth place. Denny was extremely frustrated. The following few races ended in the same way: a very poor finish.

"I like the guys," he told us at dinner when he was home for a stretch. "They're good people, but they're not a good pit crew. They're making mistakes, killing our season. If they would just give me a chance to finish, I'd finish well."

"Can't you get a new crew?" Eve asked.

I was in the kitchen, next to the dining room. I never stayed in the dining room when they ate, out of respect. No one likes a dog under the table looking for crumbs when they're eating. So I couldn't see them, but I could hear them. Denny picking up the wooden salad bowl and serving himself more salad. Zoë pushing her chicken nuggets around on the plate.

"Eat them, honey," Eve said. "Don't play with them."

"It's not the quality of the man," Denny tried to explain. "It's the quality of the team."

"How do you fix it?" Eve asked. "You're spending so much time away, it seems like a waste. What's the point of racing if you can't finish? Zoë, you've only had two bites. Eat."

The crunching of romaine. Zoë drinking from her sippy cup.

"Practice," Denny said. "Practice, practice, practice."

"When will you practice?"

"They want me to go down to Sonoma next week, work with the Apex Porsche people at Infineon. Work hard with the pit crew so there are no more mistakes. The sponsors are getting frustrated."

Eve fell silent. "Next week is your week off," she said finally.

"I won't be gone long. Three or four days. Good salad. Did you make the dressing yourself?"

I couldn't read their body language because I couldn't see them, but there are some things a dog can sense. Tension. Fear. Anxiety. From my position on the kitchen floor, I could sense Eve's anger. Clearly, she had steeled herself for Denny's racing absences; she was not prepared for his practices in Sonoma, and she was angry and afraid.

I heard chair legs scrape as a chair was pushed back. I heard plates being stacked, flatware nervously gathered.

"Eat your nuggets," Eve said again, this time sternly.

"I'm full," Zoë declared.

"You haven't eaten anything. How can you be full?" said Eve.

"I don't like nuggets."

"You're not leaving the table until you eat your nuggets."

"*I don't like nuggets!*" Zoë shrieked, and suddenly

the world was a very dark place. Anxiety. Anticipation. Excitement. All these emotions have a distinctive smell, many of which were coming from the dining room at that moment.

After a long silence, Denny said, "I'll make her a hot dog."

"No, you won't! She likes the nuggets; she's just doing this because you're here. I'm not making a new dinner every time she decides she doesn't like something. She asked for the nuggets, now she'll eat the nuggets!"

Fury has a very distinctive smell, too.

Zoë started to cry. I went to the door and looked in. Eve was standing at the head of the table, her face red and pinched. Zoë was sobbing into her nuggets. Denny stood to make himself seem bigger. It's important for the head of a pack to be bigger. Often just acting tough can get a member of the pack to back down.

"You're overreacting," he said. "Why don't you go lie down and let me finish up here."

"You always take her side!" Eve barked.

"I just want her to have a dinner she'll eat."

"Fine," Eve hissed. "I'll make her a hot dog, then."

Eve whirled from the table and almost crushed me when she burst into the kitchen. She threw open the freezer door and snatched a package of hot dogs. She grabbed a knife from the block and stabbed into the package, and that's when the evening turned really bad. As if the knife had a will of its own, the blade leapt from the frozen package and sliced deep and clean into Eve's left palm, between her thumb and fingers.

The knife clattered into the sink, and Eve grabbed her hand with a wail. Watery drops of blood speckled the counter. Denny was there in a moment with a dishcloth.

"Let me see it," he said, peeling the blood-soaked cloth from her hand, which she held by the wrist as if it were no longer a part of her body but some alien creature that had attacked her.

"We should take you to the hospital," he said.

"No!" she bellowed. "No hospital!"

"You need stitches," he said, examining the gushing wound.

She didn't answer immediately, but her eyes were filled with tears. Not from pain, but from fear. She was so afraid of doctors and hospitals. She was afraid that she might go in and they would never let her out. "Please," she whispered to Denny. "Please. No hospital."

He groaned and shook his head. "I'll see if I can close it," he said.

Zoë stood next to me, silent, eyes wide, holding a chicken nugget, watching. Neither of us knew what to do.

"Zoë, baby," Denny said. "Can you find the bandages for me in the hall closet? We'll get Mommy all patched up, okay?"

When Zoë returned with the box of bandages, she didn't know where her parents had gone, so I walked her to the bathroom door and barked. Denny opened the door a crack and took the bandages. "Thanks, Zoë. I'll take care of Mommy, now. You can go play or watch TV." He closed the door.

Zoë looked at me for a moment with concern in her eyes, and I wanted to help her. I walked toward the living room and looked back. She still hesitated, so I went to get her. I nudged her and tried again; this time she followed me. I sat before the television and waited for her to turn it on, which she did. And we watched *Kids Next Door*. And then Denny and Eve appeared.

They saw us watching TV together, and they seemed somehow relieved. They sat next to Zoë and watched along with us, not saying a word. When the show was over, Eve pressed the mute button on the remote.

"The cut isn't very bad," she said to Zoë. "If you're still hungry, I can make you a hot dog. . . ."

Zoë shook her head. And then Eve started sobbing.

"I'm so sorry," she cried. Denny put his arm around

her shoulder and held her.

"I don't want to be like this," she sobbed. "It's not me. I'm so sorry. I don't want to be mean. It's not who I am."

Beware, I thought. *The zebra hides everywhere.*

Zoë grabbed her mother and held tight, which unleashed a flood of tears from both of them, and they were joined by Denny, who hovered over them like a firefighting helicopter, dumping his bucket of tears on the fire.

I left. Not because I felt they wanted their privacy, believe me. I left because I felt that they had resolved their issues and all was good in the world. And, also, I was hungry. I wandered into the dining room and scanned the floor for droppings. There wasn't much. But in the kitchen I found something good. A nugget.

Zoë must have dropped it after Eve cut herself. I sniffed the nugget, and I recoiled in disgust. It was bad! I sniffed again. Foul. Disease laden. This nugget—and probably all the others on the plate—had definitely turned bad.

I felt sorry for Zoë: all she'd had to do was say that the nuggets didn't taste right, and this incident would have been avoided.

In racing, they say that your car goes where your eyes go. The driver who cannot tear his eyes away from the wall as he spins out of control will meet that wall; the driver who looks down the track as he feels his tires break free will regain control of his vehicle.

Your car goes where your eyes go. Simply another way of saying that you make your own destiny.

I know it's true; racing doesn't lie.

fourteen

When Denny went away the following week, we went to Eve's parents' house so they could take care of us. Eve's hand was bandaged up, which indicated to me that the cut was worse than she had let on. But it didn't slow her down much.

Maxwell and Trish, the Twins, lived in a very fancy house on a large parcel of wooded land on Mercer Island. It had an amazing view of Lake Washington and Seattle. And for having such a beautiful place to live, they were among the most unhappy people I've ever met. Nothing was good enough for them. They were always complaining about how things could be better. When we arrived, they started in about Denny right away. *He doesn't spend enough time with Zoë. He's neglecting Eve. His dog needs a bath.* Like my cleanliness had anything to do with it.

"What are you going to do?" Maxwell asked Eve.

They were standing around in the kitchen while Trish cooked dinner, making something that Zoë would inevitably hate. It was a warm spring evening, so the Twins were wearing polo shirts with their slacks. Maxwell and Trish were drinking Manhattan cocktails with cherries, Eve, a glass of wine.

"I'm going to get in shape," Eve said. "I feel fat."

"I mean about Denny," Maxwell said.

"What do I need to do about Denny?" Eve asked.

"*Something!* What is he contributing to your family?" said Trish. "*You* make all the money!"

"He's my husband and he's Zoë's father, and I love him," replied Eve. "What else does he need to contribute to our family?"

Maxwell snorted and slapped the counter. I flinched. "You're scaring the dog," Trish pointed out. She rarely called me by name.

"I'm just frustrated," Maxwell said. "I want the best for my girls. Whenever you come to stay here, it's because he's gone racing. It's not good for you."

"This season is really important for his career," Eve said, trying to remain steadfast. "I wish I were able to be more involved, but I'm doing the best I can, and he appreciates that. What I don't need is you going after me for it."

"I'm sorry," Maxwell said, holding up his hands in surrender. "I'm sorry. I just want what's best for you."

"I know, Daddy," Eve said, and she leaned forward and kissed his cheek. "I want what's best for me, too."

She took her wine outside into the backyard, and I lingered. Maxwell opened the refrigerator and retrieved a jar of the hot peppers he liked to eat. He opened the jar and squeezed his fingers inside, took one, and crunched into it.

"The dog is watching you," Trish said after a moment. "Maybe he wants a pepper."

Maxwell's expression changed.

"Want a treat, boy?" he asked, holding out a hot pepper. That wasn't why I had been watching him. I was watching him to better understand the meaning of his words. Still, I was hungry, so I sniffed at the pepper.

"They're good," he prompted. "Imported from Italy."

I took the pepper from him and immediately felt a prickly sensation on my tongue. I bit down, and a burning liquid filled my mouth. I quickly swallowed and thought I was done with the discomfort. I thought surely the acid in my stomach would cancel out the acid of the pepper. But that's when the pain really began. My throat felt as if it had been scraped raw. My stomach churned. I immediately left the room and the house. Outside the back door, I lapped at my bowl of water, but it did little to help. I made my way to a nearby shrub and lay down in its shade and rested until the burning went away.

That night Trish and Maxwell took me out, as Zoë and Eve had long been asleep. They stood at the back porch and repeated their silly saying, "Get busy, boy, get busy!" Still feeling somewhat queasy, I ventured away from the house farther than I usually did, crouched in my stance, and went. After I did my business, I saw that it was loose and watery, and when I sniffed at it, it was unusually foul-smelling. I knew I was safe and the ordeal had passed; still, since that time I have never accepted food from someone I didn't fully trust.

fifteen

The weeks tripped by with tremendous haste. There was no letup: Denny got his first victory in Laguna in early June, then third place at Road Atlanta, and he finished eighth in Denver. That week with the boys in Sonoma had worked out the kinks with the crew, and it was all on Denny's shoulders. And his shoulders were broad.

That summer, when we gathered around the dinner table, there was something to talk about. Trophies. Photographs. Replays on television late at night. Suddenly people were hanging around, coming over for dinner. Not just Mike from work but others, too. We were even introduced to Luca Pantoni, a very powerful man at Ferrari headquarters in Maranello. I never broke my rule about staying out of the dining room. I have too much integrity for that. But I sat upon the threshold, I assure you. My toenails edged over the line so that I could be that much closer to greatness. I learned more about racing in those few weeks than I had in all my years of watching video and television.

Zoë chattered away constantly, always something to say, always something to show. She would sit on Denny's knee with her big eyes, absorbing every word of the conversation. Then, at an appropriate moment she would declare some racing truth Denny had taught her—"slow hands in the fast stuff, fast hands in the slow stuff"—and all the big men would be impressed. I was proud of her in those moments; since I was unable to impress the racing men with my own knowledge, the next best thing was to experience it through Zoë.

Eve was happy again: she took what she called "mat" classes and gained muscle tone. Her health had greatly improved with no explanation: no more headaches, no more nausea. She and Denny seemed to be happy together like in the old days.

Yet for every peak there is a valley. Denny's next race was very important. A good finish would solidify his position as rookie of the year. In that race, at Phoenix International Raceway, Denny got into a crash at the first turn. This is a rule of racing: No race has ever been won in the first turn, but many have been lost there.

He got caught in a bad spot. Someone tried to pass him going into the turn and his brakes locked up. Tires don't work if they aren't rolling. In full-out skid, the other car slammed into Denny's left front wheel, destroying the car's alignment. The front of the car was skewed so badly that his car crabbed up the track, taking seconds off his lap time.

Alignment, brake lockup, crabbing—mere jargon. What matters is that Denny's car was broken. He finished the race, but he finished dead last.

"It just doesn't seem fair," Eve said. "It was the other driver's fault."

"If it was anybody's fault," Denny said, "it was mine for being where I could let it happen."

This is something I'd heard him say before: getting angry at another driver for a driving incident is pointless. You need to watch the drivers around you, understand their skill, confidence, and aggression levels, and drive with them accordingly. Know who is driving next to you. Any problems that may occur have ultimately been caused by you, because you are responsible for where you are and what you are doing there.

Still, fault or no, Denny was crushed. Zoë was crushed. Eve was crushed. I was, too. We had come so close to greatness. We had smelled it, and it smelled like roast pig.

Everybody likes the smell of roast pig. But what is worse, smelling the roast and not feasting, or not smelling the roast at all?

August was hot and dry, and the grass all around the neighborhood was brown and dead. Denny spent his time doing math. By his figuring, it was still possible for him to finish in the top ten in the series and likely win rookie of the year. Either result would assure him of getting another ride the following year.

We sat on the back porch basking in the early evening sun, the smell of Denny's freshly baked oatmeal cookies wafting from the kitchen. Zoë running in the sprinkler. Denny massaging Eve's hand gently, giving it life. I was on the deck doing my best impression of an iguana. Soaking up all the heat I could to warm my blood, hoping that if I absorbed enough, it would carry me through the winter. And it would likely be a cold, dark, and bitter winter, as a hot Seattle summer usually signifies.

"I miss you when you're not here," Eve said.

"So come with me next week," replied Denny. "Zoë will love it; we'll stay where they have a pool. She loves anything with a pool. And you can come to the track for the race."

"I can't go to the track," Eve said. "Not now. I mean, I wish I could, I really do. But I've been feeling good lately, you know? And . . . I'm afraid. The track is so loud, and it's hot, and it smells like rubber and gas, and the radio blasts static into my ears, and everyone's shouting at each other so they can be heard. It might give me a— I might react badly to it."

Denny smiled and sighed. Even Eve cracked a smile.

"Do you understand?" she asked.

"I do," Denny answered.

I did, too. Everything about the track. The sounds, the smells. Walking through the paddock, the inner circle of the track where they work on the cars. Feeling the energy, the heat of race motors coming from each pit. The electricity that ripples up and down the paddock when the announcer calls the next race group to start up. Watching the frantic scramble of the start, and then imagining the possibilities. Denny and I fed off it; it gave us life. But I totally understood that what filled us with energy could be irritating to someone else, especially Eve.

Denny and Eve looked out to the lawn and I looked with them and we all watched Zoë, her wet hair clinging to her shoulders in glistening locks. Her childish bikini and tanned feet. She ran circles around the sprinkler, her shrieks and squeals and laughs echoing through the Central District streets.

Sixteen

Your car goes where your eyes go.

We went to Denny Creek, not because it was named after Denny—it wasn't—but because it was such an enjoyable hike. With Zoë clumping along in her first pair of waffle stompers, me cut loose of my leash. Summer in the Cascades is always pleasant and cool under the canopy of cedars and alders. The beaten path is packed down, making long strides easy. Off the beaten path—where dogs prefer—is a soft and spongy bed of fallen needles.

And the smell! Richness and fertility. Growth and death and food and decay. Waiting. Just waiting for someone to smell it, lingering close to the ground in layers. A good nose like mine can separate each odor to identify and enjoy each distinct scent. I rarely let myself go, practicing to be restrained like men are. But that day, I ran through those woods wildly, like a crazy dog. Diving through the bushes, over the fallen trees, giving gentle chase to chipmunks, barking at the jays. Rolling over and scratching my back on the sticks and leaves and needles and earth.

We made our way along the path, up the hills and down, eventually arriving at the Slippery Slabs, as they are called. Where the creek runs over a series of broad, flat rocks, pooling at some points, streaming at others. Kids love the Slippery Slabs as they slide through the stream.

And so we arrived and I drank the water, cold and fresh, the last of that year's snowmelt. Zoë and Denny and Eve stripped down to their swimsuits and bathed gently in the waters. Zoë was old enough to slide by herself, and Denny took the lower and Eve took the upper and they slid Zoë down the stream of water, Eve giving a push and Zoë slipping down. The rocks weren't slippery when dry, but when wet, there was a film on them that made them quite slick. Down she would go, squealing and squirming, splashing into the frigid pool at Denny's feet; he would snatch her up and whisk her back to Eve, who would slide her down again. And again.

People, like dogs, love repetition. Chasing a ball, going around a track in a race car, sliding down a slide. Because as much as each incident is similar, so it is different. Denny and Eve passed Zoë back and forth safely between them.

Until once. Eve dipped Zoë into the stream, and Zoë suddenly pulled her toes from the icy water, upsetting Eve's balance. Eve shifted her weight and managed to set Zoë down safely on the dry rock, but her move was too quick. Her foot touched the creek, and she didn't realize how slippery those rocks were, slippery slabs like glass.

Her legs went out from underneath her. She reached out, but her hand grasped only the air; her fist closed, empty. Her head hit the rock with a loud crack and bounced. It hit and bounced and hit again, like a rubber ball. We stood, it seemed like for a long time, waiting to see what was going to happen. Eve lay unmoving, and there was Zoë, again the cause, not knowing what to do. She looked at her father, who quickly bounded up to them both.

"Are you okay?"

Eve blinked hard, painfully. There was blood in her mouth. "I bit my tongue," she said woozily.

"How's your head?" Denny asked.

"—Hurts."

"Can you make it back to the car?" With me in the lead herding Zoë, Denny steered Eve. She wasn't staggering, but she was lost, and who knows where she would have ended up if someone hadn't been with her. It was early evening when we got to the hospital in Bellevue.

"You probably have a minor concussion," Denny said.

"But they should check it out."

"I'm okay," Eve repeated over and over. But clearly she wasn't okay. She was dazed and slurring her words and she kept nodding off. Denny would wake her up, saying something about not falling asleep when you have a concussion. They all went inside and left me in the car with the windows open a crack. I settled into the pocket-like passenger seat of Denny's car and forced myself to sleep.

seventeen

In Mongolia, when a dog dies, he is buried high in the hills so people cannot walk on his grave. The dog's master whispers into the dog's ear his wishes that the dog will return as a man in his next life. Then a piece of meat or fat is placed in his mouth to sustain his soul on its journey. Before he comes back to life as a man, the dog's soul is freed to travel the land, to run across the high desert plains for as long as it would like.

I learned that from a program on the National Geographic Channel, so I believe it is true. Not all dogs return as men, they say; only those who are ready.

I am ready.

eighteen

It was hours before Denny returned, and he returned alone. He let me out, and I could barely scramble from the seat before unleashing a torrent of urine on the lamppost in front of me.

"Sorry, boy," he said. "I didn't forget about you."

When I had finished, he opened a package of peanut butter sandwich crackers he must have gotten from a vending machine. I love those crackers the best. It's the salt and the butter in the crackers mixed with the fat in the peanuts. I tried to eat slowly, savoring each bite, but I was too hungry and swallowed them so quickly I barely got to taste them. What a shame to waste something so wonderful on a dog. Sometimes I hate what I am so much.

We sat by the parking lot for quite a long time, not speaking or anything. He seemed upset, and when he was upset, I knew the best thing I could do was be available for him. So I lay next to him and waited. Denny and I sat at length and watched the people coming and going from the parking lot. We did nothing more than breathe. We did not need conversation to communicate with each other. After a while, a car pulled into the parking lot and parked near us. It was a beautiful Alfa Romeo in mint condition. Mike got out slowly and walked toward us.

I greeted him, and he gave me a perfunctory pat on the head. He continued over to Denny and sat down in my spot on the bench. "I appreciate this, Mike," Denny said.

"Hey, man, no problem," said Mike. "What about Zoë?"

"Eve's dad took her to their house and put her to bed," replied Denny.

Mike nodded. The crickets were louder than the traffic from the nearby Interstate 405, but not by much. We listened to them, a concert of crickets, wind, leaves, cars, and fans on the roof of the hospital building.

Here's why I will be a good person. Because I listen. I cannot speak, so I listen very well. I never interrupt, I never change the course of the conversation with a comment of my own. People, if you pay attention to them, change the direction of one another's conversations constantly. It's like having a passenger in your car who suddenly grabs the steering wheel and turns you down a side street. Learn to listen! I beg of you. Pretend you are a dog like me and listen to other people rather than steal their stories.

I listened that night and I heard.

"How long will they keep Eve?" Mike asked.

"They might not even do a test," said Denny. "They might just go in and take it out. Cancer or not, it's still causing problems. The headaches, the nausea, the mood swings."

"Sorry," Mike said. "I'm . . . sorry." He grabbed me by the scruff and gave me a shake. "Really rough," he said. "I'd be freaking out right now if I were you."

Denny stood up tall. For him. He wasn't a tall guy. He was a Formula One guy. Well proportioned and powerful, but scaled down. A flyweight.

"I am freaking out," he said.

Mike nodded thoughtfully.

"You don't look it. I guess that's why you're such a good driver," he said, and I looked at him quickly. That was just what I was thinking.

"You don't mind stopping by my place and getting his stuff?"

Denny took out his key ring, picked through the bundle.

"The food is in the pantry. Give him a cup and a half. He gets three of those chicken cookies before he goes to bed—take his bed, it's in the bedroom. And take his dog. Just say, 'Where's your dog?' and he'll find it, sometimes he hides it."

He found the house key and held it out for Mike, letting the other keys dangle. "It's the same for both locks," he said.

"We'll be fine," Mike said. "Do you want me to bring you some clothes?"

"No," Denny said. "I'll go back in the morning and pack a bag if we're staying."

No words, then, just crickets, wind, traffic, fans blowing on the roof, a distant siren. "You don't have to keep it inside," Mike said. "You can let go. We're in a parking lot."

Denny looked up at Mike. "This is why she didn't want to go to the hospital."

"What?" Mike asked.

"This is what she was afraid of," said Denny. Mike nodded, but clearly he didn't understand what Denny was saying.

"What about your race next week?" he asked.

"I'll call Jonny tomorrow and tell him I'm out for the season," Denny said. "I have to be *here*."

Mike took me to our house to get my things. I was humiliated when he said, "Where's your dog?" I didn't want to admit that I still slept with a stuffed animal. But I did. I loved that dog, and Denny was right, I did hide it during the day because I didn't want Zoë to add it to her collection. And also, I was afraid of the virus that had possessed the zebra.

But I got my dog out of his hiding spot under the sofa and we climbed back into Mike's Alfa and went to his house. His partner asked how it all went, and Mike brushed him off right away and poured himself a drink.

"That guy is bottled so tight," Mike said. "He's gonna have a heart attack or something."

Mike's partner Tony picked up my dog that I had dropped on the floor. "We have to take this, too?" he asked.

"Listen," Mike sighed, "everyone needs a security blanket. What's wrong with that?"

"It stinks," Mike's partner said. "I'll wash it." And he put it in the washing machine! My dog! He took the first toy that Denny ever gave me and stuck it into the washing machine . . . with soap! I couldn't believe it. I was stunned. No one had ever handled my dog in such a way!

I watched through the glass window of the machine as it spun around and around, sloshing with the suds. And they laughed at me. Not meanly. They thought I was a dumb dog—all people do. They laughed and I watched and when it came out, they put it in the dryer with a towel, and I waited. And when it was dry, they took it out and gave it to me. Tony took it out and it was warm, and he handed it to me and said, "Much better, right?"

When Tony handed me my dog, I took it in my mouth out of respect. I took it to my bed because that's what Denny would have wanted me to do. And I curled up with it. And the funny part? I liked it.

I liked my stuffed dog better clean than smelly, which was something I never would have imagined. But which gave me something I could hold on to. A belief that the center of our family could not be changed by a chance occurrence, an accidental washing, an unexpected illness. Deep in the center of our family existed a bond; Denny, Zoë, Eve, me, and even my stuffed dog. However things might change around us, we would always be together.

nineteen

I was not always included, being a dog. I was not allowed into the hospital to hear the hushed conversations. To witness the doctor with the blue hat and blue gown whispering his opinions and misgivings. Revealing the clues they all should have seen, explaining the mysteries of the brain. No one confided in me. I was never consulted. Nothing was expected of me except that I do my business outside when called upon to do so, and that I stop barking when told to stop barking.

Eve stayed in the hospital for a long time. Weeks. Because there was so much for Denny to do, caring for both me and Zoë, as well as visiting Eve in the hospital whenever possible, he decided that the best plan was to start living by a system, rather than our usual spontaneous way of living.

At the end of the workday, Denny retrieved Zoë from camp and returned home to cook dinner while Zoë watched cartoons. After dinner, Denny gave me my food and then took Zoë to visit Eve. Later, they returned, Denny bathed Zoë, read her a story, and tucked her into bed. Weekends were spent largely at the hospital. It was not a very colorful way to live. My walks were infrequent, my trips to the dog park nonexistent. Little attention was paid to me by Denny or Zoë. But I was ready to make that sacrifice in the interest of Eve's well-being. I vowed not to be a squeaky wheel in any way.

After two weeks of this pattern, Maxwell and Trish offered to keep Zoë for a weekend, so as to give Denny a bit of a break. They told him he looked sickly, that he should take a vacation from his troubles, and Eve agreed. "I don't want to see you this weekend," she said to him, at least that's what he told Zoë and me. Denny had mixed feelings about the idea. I could tell as he packed Zoë's overnight bag. He was hesitant to let Zoë go. But he did let her go, and then he and I were alone. And it felt very strange.

We did all the things we used to do. We went jogging.

We ordered delivery pizza for lunch. We spent the afternoon watching a fantastic racing movie. After that, Denny took me to the Blue Dog Park that was a few blocks away, and he threw the ball for me. But even for that venture, our energy was wrong; a vicious dog got after me and was at my throat with bared teeth everywhere I moved. I couldn't retrieve the tennis ball but was forced to stay close by Denny's side.

It all felt wrong. The absence of Eve and Zoë was wrong. There was something missing in everything we did. After we had both eaten dinner, we sat together in the kitchen, fidgeting. There was nothing for us to do but fidget. Because while we were going through the motions, doing what we always used to do, there was no joy in it whatsoever.

Finally, Denny stood. He took me outside, and I urinated for him. He gave me my usual bedtime cookies, and then he said to me, "You be good."

He said, "I have to go see her." I followed him to the door; I wanted to go see her, too.

"No," he said to me. "You stay here. They won't let you into the hospital."

I understood; I went to my bed and lay down.

"Thanks, Enzo," he said. And then he left.

He returned a few hours later, in the darkness, and he silently climbed into his bed with a shiver before the sheets got warm. I lifted my head and he saw me.

"She's going to be okay," he said to me. "She's going to be okay."

twenty

Zoë and me, playing in the backyard on a sunny afternoon. She made me wear the bumblebee wings she had worn the previous Halloween. She dressed herself in her pink ballet outfit with the puffy skirt and the leotard and tights. We went out into the backyard and ran around together until her pink feet were stained with dirt.

It was the Tuesday after her weekend with Maxwell and Trish, and by then she had thankfully lost the sour vinegar smell that clung to her whenever she spent time at the Twins' house. Denny had left work early and picked up Zoë so they could go shopping for new sneakers and socks. When they got home, Denny cleaned the house while Zoë and I played. We danced and laughed and ran and pretended we were angels.

She called me over to the corner of the yard by the spigot. On the wood chips lay one of her Barbie dolls. She kneeled down before it. "You're going to be okay," she said to the doll. "Everything is going to be okay."

She unfolded a dishcloth that she'd brought from the house. In the dishcloth were scissors, a Sharpie pen, and masking tape. She pulled off the doll's head. She took the kitchen scissors and cut off Barbie's hair, down to the plastic nub. She then drew a line on the doll's skull, all the while whispering softly, "Everything's going to be okay."

When she was done, she tore off a piece of masking tape and put it on the doll's head. She pressed the head back onto the neck stub and laid the doll down. We both stared at it. A moment of silence. "Now she can go to heaven," Zoë said to me. "And I'll live with Grandma and Grandpa."

I was sad. Clearly, the weekend of rest Maxwell and Trish had offered Denny was a false one. I had no clear evidence, and yet I could sense it. For the Twins, it had been a working weekend, an effort to establish a plot. They were already sowing the seeds of their story, spinning their lies, foretelling a future they hoped would come true.

twenty-one

Soon, Labor Day weekend came, and after that, Zoë was enrolled in school. "Real school," as she called it. Kindergarten. And she was so excited to go. She picked out her clothes the night before her first day, bell-bottom jeans and sneakers and a bright yellow blouse. She had her backpack, her lunch box, her pencil case, her notebook. With great ceremony, Denny and I walked with her a block from our house to the corner of Martin Luther King Jr. Way, and we waited for the bus that would take her to her new elementary school. We waited with a few other kids and parents from the neighborhood.

When the bus came over the hill, we were all so excited.

"Kiss me now," she said to Denny.

"Now?" he replied.

"Not when the bus is here. I don't want Jessie to see."

Jessie was her best friend from preschool, who was going to be in the same kindergarten class. Denny obliged and kissed her before the bus had stopped.

"After school, you go to Extended Day," he said. "Like we practiced yesterday at orientation. Remember?"

"*Daddy!*" she scolded.

Denny said, "I'll pick you up after Extended Day. You wait in the classroom, and I'll come and get you."

"Daddy!" She made a stern face at him, and for a second I could have sworn she was Eve. The flashing eyes. The flared nostrils. The head cocked, ready for battle. She quickly turned and climbed onto the bus. Then, as she walked down the aisle, she turned and waved at us both before she took her seat ncxt to her friend.

The bus pulled away and headed for school. "Your first?" another father asked Denny.

"Yeah," Denny replied. "My only. You?"

"My third," the man said. "But there's nothing like your first. They grow up so fast."

"That they do," Denny said with a smile; we turned and walked home.

twenty-two

It was an evening on which Denny took me along to the hospital to visit Eve, though I didn't get to go inside. After the visit, Zoë and I waited in the car while Maxwell and Trish joined Denny to talk on the pavement. Zoë was immersed in a book of mazes, something she loved to do; I listened carefully to the conversation. Everything they said made sense, but none of it added up properly in my mind. Maxwell and Trish did all of the talking.

"Of course, there has to be a nurse on duty, around the clock."

"They work in shifts—"

"They work in shifts, but still, the one on duty takes breaks."

"So someone needs to be there to help."

"And since we're always around . . ."

"We have nowhere to go—"

"And you have to work."

"So it's best."

"Yes, it's best."

Denny nodded without conviction. He got into the car, and we drove off. "When's Mommy coming home?" Zoë asked.

"Soon," Denny said. We were crossing the floating bridge, the one Zoë used to call the "High 90," when she was younger. "Mommy's going to stay with Grandma and Grandpa for a while," Denny said. "Until she feels better. Is that okay with you?"

"I guess," Zoë said. "Why?"

"It'll be easier for—" He broke off. "It'll be easier."

A few days later, a Saturday, Zoë, Denny, and I went to Maxwell and Trish's house. A bed had been set up in the living room. A large hospital bed that moved up and down and tilted and did all sorts of things by touching a remote control. It had a broad footboard from which hung a clipboard. There was also a nurse, a crinkly older woman who had a voice that sounded like she was singing whenever she spoke. And who didn't like dogs, though I had no objection to her whatsoever. Immediately, the nurse started fretting about me. To my dismay, Maxwell agreed and Denny didn't notice, so I was shoved outside into the backyard; thankfully, Zoë came to my rescue.

"Mommy's coming!" Zoë told me. She was very excited and wore the plaid dress that she liked because it was so pretty. I felt her excitement, too, so I joined in with it. I embraced the festivity, a real homecoming. Zoë and I played; she threw a ball for me and I did tricks for her, and we rolled together in the grass. It was a wonderful day, the family all together again. It felt very special.

"She's here!" Denny called from the back door, and Zoë and I rushed to see; this time I was allowed inside. Eve's mother entered the house first, followed by a man in blue slacks and a yellow shirt with a logo on it. He wheeled in a white figure with dead eyes, a mannequin in slippers. Maxwell and Denny lifted the figure and placed it in the bed. The nurse tucked it in and Zoë said, "Hi, Mommy," and all this happened before it even entered my mind that this strange figure was not a dummy, not a mock-up used for practice, but Eve.

Her head was covered with a stocking cap. Her cheeks were sunken, her skin, sallow. She lifted her head and looked around. "I feel like a Christmas tree," she said. "In the living room, everyone standing around me expecting something. I don't have any presents." Uncomfortable chuckles from the onlookers.

And then she looked at me directly. "Enzo," she said. "Come here." I wagged my tail and approached cautiously. I hadn't seen her since she went into the hospital, and I wasn't prepared for what I saw. It seemed to me the hospital had made her much sicker than she really was.

"He doesn't know what to think," Denny said for me.

"It's okay, Enzo," she said.

She dangled her hand off the side of the bed, and I bumped it with my nose. I didn't like any of this, all the new furniture, Eve looking limp and sad, people standing around like Christmas without the presents. None of it seemed right. So even though everyone was staring at me, I shuffled over to Zoë and stood behind her, looking out the windows into the backyard, which was dappled with sunlight.

"I think I've offended him by being sick," she said.

That was not what I meant at all. My feelings were so complicated, I have difficulty explaining them clearly even today, after I have lived through it and had time to think about it. All I could do was move to her bedside and lie down before her like a rug.

"I don't like seeing me like this either," she said.

The afternoon went on forever. Finally the dinner hour came, and Maxwell, Trish, and Denny poured themselves cocktails and the mood lifted greatly. An old photo album of Eve as a child was taken out from hiding and everyone laughed while the smell of garlic and oil floated from the kitchen, where Trish cooked the food. Eve showered with the help of the nurse. When she emerged from the bathroom in one of her own dresses and not the hospital gown and robe, she looked almost normal. Except there was a darkness behind her eyes, a look like she had given up. She tried to read Zoë a book, but she said she couldn't focus well enough, so Zoë tried her best to read to Eve, and her best was fairly good. I wandered into the kitchen, where Denny was again talking with Trish and Maxwell.

"We really think Zoë should stay with us," Maxwell said, "until . . ."

"Until . . . ," Trish echoed, standing at the stove with her back to us.

So much of language is unspoken. So much of language is made of looks and gestures. Trish's robotic repeating of the single word "*until*" revealed everything about her state of mind.

"Until *what*?" Denny demanded. I could hear the irritation in his voice. "How do you know what's going to happen? You're condemning her to something before you even know."

Trish dropped her frying pan onto the burner with a

loud clatter and began to sob. Maxwell wrapped his arms around her and enveloped her in his embrace. He looked over at Denny.

"Please, Denny. We have to face the reality of it. The doctor said six to eight months. He was quite definite."

Trish pulled away from him and steadied herself, sniffed in her tears. "My baby," she whispered.

"Zoë is just a child," Maxwell continued. "This is valuable time—the *only* time she has to spend with Eve. I can't *imagine*—I can't *believe for a second*—that you would possibly object."

"You're such a caring person," Trish added.

I could see that Denny was stuck. He had agreed to have Eve stay with Maxwell and Trish, and now they wanted Zoë, too. If he objected, he would be keeping a mother and a daughter apart. If he accepted their proposal, he would be pushed away. He would become an outsider in his own family.

"I understand what you're saying—," Denny said.

"We knew you would," Trish interrupted.

"But I'll have to talk to Zoë about it to see what she wants."

Trish and Maxwell looked at each other uneasily. "You can't seriously consider asking a little girl what she wants," Maxwell snorted. "She's *five*, for heaven's sake! She can't—"

"I'll talk to Zoë to see what she wants," Denny repeated firmly.

After dinner, he took Zoë into the backyard, and they sat together on the terrace steps. "Mommy would like it if you stayed here with her and Grandma and Grandpa," he said. "What do you think about that?"

She turned it over in her head.

"What do *you* think about it?" she asked.

"Well," Denny said, "I think maybe it's the best thing. Mommy has missed you so much, and she wants to spend more time with you. It would just be for a little while. Until she's better and can come home."

"Oh," Zoë said. "I still get to take the bus to school?"

"Well," Denny said, thinking. "Probably not. Not for a while. Grandma or Grandpa will drive you to school and pick you up, I think. When Mommy feels better, you both will come home, then you can take the bus again."

"Oh," said Zoë.

"I'll come and visit every day," Denny said. "And we'll spend weekends together, and sometimes you'll stay with me, too. But Mommy really wants you with her."

Zoë nodded somberly.

"Grandma and Grandpa really want me, too," she said.

Denny was clearly upset, but he was hiding it in a way that I thought little kids didn't understand. But Zoë was very smart, like her father. Even at five years old, she understood.

"It's okay, Daddy," she said. "I know you won't leave me here forever."

He smiled at her and took her little-kid hand and held it in his own and kissed her on the forehead.

"I promise I will never do that," he said. It was agreed then that she would stay.

As the night wound down, I found Denny sitting in the stuffed chair next to Eve's bed, nervously tapping his hand against his leg.

"Denny, please—"

There was something about the tone of her voice, something pleading in her eyes, that made him stop. "Please go home," she said. He scratched the back of his neck and looked down. "I don't want you to see me like this."

"Like what?" said Denny.

"Look at me," she said. "My head is shaved. My face looks old. My breath smells bad. I'm ugly—"

"I don't care what you look like," he said. "I see who you really are."

"*I* care what I look like," she said, trying to muster her old Eve smile. "When I look at you, I see my reflection in your eyes. I don't want to be ugly in front of you."

Denny turned away as if to shield his eyes from her.

"I'll pack Zoë's things and come back in the morning," he said, finally, without turning around.

"Thank you, Denny," Eve said, relieved. He kissed Eve good night, tucked Zoë into bed, and then he left. I was surprised when he left me with Eve. I hadn't realized I was part of the package.

The house grew quiet and dark, Zoë in bed, Maxwell and Trish in their room with their TV blinking under the door. Eve was settled into her bed in the living room with the nurse sitting in a dark corner playing a page of her word-search book, in which she circled the hidden messages. I lay next to Eve's bed.

Later, Eve was asleep and the nurse nudged me with her foot. I lifted my head and she held a finger to her lips and told me to be a good dog and follow her, which I did. She led me through the kitchen, through the laundry room to the back of the house, and she opened the door that led to the garage.

"In you go," she said. "We don't want you disturbing Mrs. Swift during the night."

I looked at her, puzzled. Disturb Eve? Why would I do that?

She took my hesitation as rebellion; she snatched my collar and gave it a jerk. She shoved me into the dark garage and closed the door. I heard her slippers tread away, back into the house.

I was not afraid. All I knew was how dark it was in the garage.

It wasn't too cold, and it wasn't overly unpleasant, if you don't mind a concrete floor and the smell of engine oil in an absolutely pitch-black room. I'm sure there were no rats, as Maxwell kept a clean garage for his valuable cars. But I had never slept in a garage before. I restlessly bided my time.

Hours into my nightmare, the garage door opened, and Eve was there in her nightgown, silhouetted by the night-light in the kitchen.

"Enzo?" she questioned.

I said nothing, but I emerged from the darkness, relieved to see her again.

"Come with me."

She led me back to the living room and she took a cushion from the sofa and placed it next to her bed. She told me to lie on it, and I did. Then she climbed into the bed and pulled up the sheets to her neck.

"I need you with me," she said. "Don't go away again."

But I hadn't gone away! I had been kidnapped!

I could feel the sleep pressing down on her.

"I need you with me," she said. "I'm so afraid. I'm so afraid."

It's okay, I said. *I'm here.* She rolled to the edge of the bed and looked down at me, her eyes glazed.

"Get me through tonight," she said. "That's all I need. Protect me. Don't let it happen tonight. Enzo, please. You're the only one who can help."

I will, I said.

"You're the only one. Don't worry about that nurse; I sent her home." I looked over to the corner, and the crinkly old woman was gone. "I don't need her," she said. "Only you can protect me. Please. Don't let it happen tonight."

I didn't sleep at all that night. I stood guard, waiting for the demon to show his face. The demon was coming for Eve, but he would have to get past me first, and I was ready. I noted every sound, every creak, every change in the air. By standing or shifting my weight, I silently made it clear to the demon that he would have to contend with me if he intended to take Eve.

The demon stayed away. In the morning, the others awoke and cared for Eve, and I was able to relinquish my guard duties and sleep.

"What a lazy dog," I heard Maxwell mutter as he passed me.

And then I felt Eve's hand on my neck, stroking.

"Thank you," she said. "Thank you."

twenty-three

For the first few weeks of our new arrangement Denny and I lived in our house, while Eve and Zoë lived with the Twins. Denny visited them every single evening after work, while I stayed home alone. By Halloween, Denny's pace had slowed, and by Thanksgiving, he visited them only twice during the week. Whenever he came home from the Twins' house, he reported to me how good Eve looked and how much better she was getting and that she would be coming home soon. But I saw her, too, on the weekends, when he would take me to visit, and I knew. She wasn't getting better, and she wouldn't be coming home any time soon.

At times that winter, all the extra driving around to make sure Zoë was where she was supposed to be at the correct time was very confusing to me. And I wasn't the

only one confused, I assure you. For while Zoë was sleeping with the Twins and Eve, they often called upon Denny
to shuttle her to and from soccer practice or ballet or birthday parties. Sometimes, Denny would receive a reminder
call before the pick-up time. Sometimes, he received the
reminder call after the scheduled pick-up time, and that
was never good. He would leap to his feet, throw on his
jacket, and run out of the house at full speed, only to
return later, scratching his head. "I'm sure they told me
five o'clock," he would say. "I could have sworn they said
five."

I know that sometimes his tardiness was due to his
forgetfulness, as he was always very tired and sad, but
it was also because of the extra hours he was working
to make up for all the time he had to take off in order to
attend to Eve.

One incident in particular drew the ire of Maxwell
and Trish above all others. Denny was supposed to pick
up Zoë from her ballet class, which was taught at a dance
studio located in a strip mall near Coal Creek, which, as
you can imagine by its name, was not a particularly scenic
place. That evening, Denny's car decided to stop working.
He called Maxwell and Trish many times to alert them
to his predicament, but, alas, he could not reach them.
Denny grew more and more frantic as the hour grew late.

Finally, he called an Orange Taxi, which was able to come to our house immediately, and together we drove across the lake to retrieve Zoë. I went too, at the insistence of the driver, who was particularly fond of dogs, though he didn't own one himself due to the allergic disposition of his wife.

We arrived at the dance studio over an hour late, and when we got there, Zoë was sitting on the pavement outside of the building with an older man. Both of them wore jackets that were too light for the weather.

"The teacher had to leave," the man said. "I'm the custodian. I told her I'd wait."

Denny thanked the man, and as we three returned to the taxi, a dark SUV squealed into the parking lot. Trish jumped out of the car and ran toward us.

"I got a call from another parent who drove by and saw Zoë sitting out on the curb," she snapped at Denny. "Oh, you poor dear, you're absolutely freezing!"

She wrapped her own coat around Zoë, enveloping her, and she guided Zoë to the waiting car, where she helped her into her booster seat in the back.

"What on earth do you think you're doing?" she hissed at Denny after the car door had closed.

"My car broke down," he said. "I tried to call."

"Well, you didn't try hard enough, did you? She is a

little girl, Denny. She should not be left to sit in a dark, cold parking lot with a janitor! You should be ashamed!"

"My car—"

"Then you should get yourself a new one. I don't know what's less dependable, your car or you. I am finished asking you to help with Zoë. Finished."

She climbed back into her very large car and drove away quickly; we returned to our taxi and went home.

This incident affected Denny very much, not because it wounded his pride, but because it interfered with his relationship with Zoë. You see, Denny missed Eve tremendously, but he missed Zoë even more. I could see it most on those days when he kept Zoë overnight and we got to walk her to her bus stop. On those mornings, our house seemed filled with electricity so that neither Denny nor I needed the alarm clock to wake. Instead we waited anxiously in the darkness until the hour came to rouse Zoë. We didn't want to miss a single minute we could spend with her.

On those mornings, Denny was a different person altogether. The way he so lovingly packed her sack lunches, often writing a note on a piece of notepaper, a thought or a joke he hoped she would find at lunch and might make her smile. The way he took such care with her peanut butter and banana sandwiches, slicing the banana so that each slice was exactly the same thickness. (I got to eat the extra banana on those occasions, which I enjoyed. I love bananas almost as much as I love pancakes, my favorite food.)

I knew it was never Denny's intent to be late to pick up Zoë. But, as on a race track, the reasons why matter less than the facts at hand. And, really, Trish was right: a little girl should not sit in a cold, dark parking lot for an hour with a janitor. Even Denny would admit that.

twenty-four

In February, the black pit of winter, we went on a trip to north-central Washington, to an area called the Methow Valley. It is important for United States citizens to celebrate the birthdays of their greatest presidents, so all the schools were closed for a week; Denny, Zoë, and I went to a cabin in the snowy mountains to celebrate. The cabin was owned by a relative of Eve's whom I had never met. It was quite cold, too cold for me, though on the warmer afternoons I enjoyed running in the snow. I much preferred to lie by the baseboard heater and let the others do their exercises—skiing and snowshoeing and all of that. Eve, who was too weak to travel, and her parents were not there. But many others were, all of whom were relatives of some kind or another. We were only there, I overheard, because Eve had thought it was very important for Zoë to spend time with these people, since she, Eve, someone said, would die very soon.

I didn't like that whole line of reasoning. First, that Eve would be dying soon. And second, that Zoë needed to spend time with people she had never met because Eve would soon die. They might have been perfectly pleasant people, in their puffy pants and fleece vests and sweaters that smelled of sweat. I don't know. But I wondered why they had waited for Eve's illness to make themselves available for companionship.

There were a great many of them, and I had no idea who was connected to whom. They were all cousins, I understood, but there were certain generational gaps that were confusing to me, and some of the people were without parents but were with uncles and aunts instead, and some might have just been friends. Zoë and Denny kept mostly to themselves, but they still participated in certain group events like horseback riding in the snow, sledding, and snowshoeing. The group meals were convivial, and though I was determined to remain aloof, one of the cousins was always willing to slip me a treat at mealtime. And no one ever kicked me out from under the very large dining table where I lingered during dinner even though I was breaking my own personal code; a certain sense of lawlessness pervaded the house, what with children staying awake late into the night and adults sleeping at all hours of the day like dogs. Why shouldn't I have partaken in the debauchery?

Conflicted though I was, each night something special happened that I liked very much. Outside the house—which had many identical rooms, each with many identical beds to house the multitude—was a stone patio with a large hearth. Apparently in the summer months, it was used for outdoor cooking, but it was used in the winter as well. I didn't care for the stones, which were very cold and were sprinkled with salt pellets that hurt when they got wedged between my pads, but I loved the hearth. Fire! Crackling and hot it blazed in the evenings after dinner, and they all gathered, bundled in their great coats, and one had a guitar and gloves without fingertips and he played music while they all sang. It was well below freezing, but I had my place next to the hearth. And the stars we could see! Billions of them, because the night was so intensely dark, and the sounds in the distance, the snap of a snow-burdened tree branch giving way to the wind. The barking of coyotes, my brethren, calling each other to the hunt. And when the cold overpowered the heat from the hearth, we all shuffled into the house and into our separate rooms, our fur and jackets smelling of smoke and pine sap and flaming marshmallows.

As the end of the week drew near, everyone had settled into their routines: certain cousins went skiing, others to the snowmobile park, and so on. Denny and Zoë preferred to go on leisurely snowshoe walks together, and they always took me. They had purchased little dog booties for me at the local lodge, and though I felt them unbecoming for a durable dog such as myself, I appreciated that they protected my paws from freezing or getting cut from the rough snow and frozen branches that lay hidden underneath.

On the final day of our stay, we went for a special walk at a place called Sun Mountain, which we drove to in Denny's car. It was a bit far and tricky to find; some of the cousins drew a map for Denny. But it was supposed to be a spectacular and glorious walk with tremendous views all around the valley.

We began our walk easily enough, finding the small parking lot, bundling up, strapping on our shoes, and heading off along a low trail. The area was quite remote and didn't seem to have been traveled recently, and so our isolation was somewhat idyllic. Eventually, the path began a switchback pattern and climbed a low mountain, leveled off, and then began a switchback again. Higher and higher we climbed, and yet, since we were in a thick forest and entirely surrounded by trees, we had little sense of our altitude. Up and up we climbed; deeper and deeper into the woods we delved, until we were quite exhausted.

"We should be getting close," Denny said to us, but he seemed unsure.

"I'm tired," Zoë complained.

"Let's just get to the top of the mountain," Denny urged. And so we continued on.

When we finally reached the mountaintop, it was all that Denny had hoped for. The view was stunning, as we could stand in one spot and turn completely around to see the entire Methow Valley spread out below us. But there was little time for enjoyment: in the distance, we could see very dark clouds forming, growing, blotting out more and more of the sky as we watched; and Zoë was crying softly, her face etched with pain.

"What's wrong, Honey?" Denny asked.

"My toes won't move," she said.

"Sure they will," he said. "Just wiggle them."

But when we looked down at her feet, Denny and I realized the problem: Zoë wasn't wearing her insulated boots. She was wearing her normal street shoes. She had forgotten to change her shoes when we left the car.

Denny became very quiet, and I knew he was thinking of all the terrible possibilities: frozen toes, frostbite, chilblains. And he was likely probing his own mind for wilderness survival tips he had picked up along his life's journey. Suddenly, he swooped Zoë into his arms and headed off down the hill.

It was not an easy trip, down a steep and snowy, little-used path. But Denny was determined to get his daughter to safety. Down we plunged, back into the valley, as the sky above our heads grew more ominous and Zoë's face registered her pain, though her words did not betray her. When we reached the car, Denny started the engine right away to get the heat going. He peeled off Zoë's shoes, and she cried out.

"That's good," he said. "If they hurt, that's good. That means they're going to be okay."

We drove the rest of the way down the mountain in great haste, and dangerously so, as the car slipped mightily on the hard-packed snow. When we reached the main road, which was bare and wet, Denny hesitated. To get us back to the cabin, he should turn north, but he turned on his blinker for a right hand turn, which was south.

"Chelan has a hospital," he said, explaining to me his actions. So we turned south toward Chelan.

I waited in the car while Denny rushed Zoë into the emergency room. It was my lot to wait in cars outside emergency rooms, I suppose. I'm not sure what good I would have been inside, anyway. So I waited and I watched as the dark storm clouds first engulfed the entire sky and then began to pelt our car with a freezing rain the likes of which I had never experienced. It was frightening, the force of this storm, with its high winds and icy bits of hail being flung about. I feared for my own life, being locked in the car as I was.

After they had been in the hospital for over an hour, suddenly, Denny emerged carrying Zoë. They ran to our car and opened the door. Denny laid Zoë on the backseat, strapped on her seat belt, and tucked her in with blankets he had taken from the hospital. Her feet were covered with many layers of socks, so they looked over-sized and incapable of carrying her. Denny told me to sit in the backseat with Zoë and keep her warm, which I did. We stopped at a gas station as we left Chelan to purchase chains for our tires. And before we started our journey again, Denny made a phone call on his cell phone.

"We're in a bit of trouble here," he said tensely. "Zoë has frostbitten toes—"

He stopped talking for a moment to allow the person to whom he was speaking—Eve, I assumed—to express herself in loud exclamations.

"Please listen," he said. "She's going to be fine. They gave us some ointment, and they gave her some pain medication; she'll be fine. But there's a terrible storm moving in and we're going to try for home. We won't even go back to the cabin to get our things. Please ask one of the cousins to bring our stuff home with them. If we don't get over the mountains right now, we could be stuck for more than a week on this side. Please don't call me; I have to concentrate on the road. I'll call you when we get home. I love you and I'm sorry. I'm very, very sorry."

He hung up the phone and off we drove.

The drive south was horrific. The freezing rain accumulated on the windshield faster than the wipers could push it away, and every few tedious miles Denny would stop the car and get out to scrape away the icy glaze. It was dangerous driving and I didn't like it at all. From the backseat with Zoë, I could see Denny's hands were gripping the steering wheel far too tightly. In a race car the hands must be relaxed, and Denny's always are when I see the in-car videos from his races; he often flexes his fingers to remind himself to relax his grip. But for that excruciating drive down the Columbia River, Denny held the wheel in a death grip.

I felt very bad for Zoë, who was clearly frightened. The rear of the car moved more suddenly than the front, and so she and I experienced more of the slipping and sliding sensation generated by the ice. Thinking of how scared Zoë must have been, I worked myself into a state of agitation, and I let myself get carried away. Before I knew it, I was in a full-blown panic. I pushed at the windows. I tried to clamber into the front seat, which was totally counterproductive. Denny finally barked, "Zoë, please settle Enzo down!"

She grabbed me around the neck and held me tightly. I fell against her as she lay back, and she started singing a song in my ear, one I remembered from her past, "Hello, little Enzo, so glad to see you. . . ." She had just started preschool when she learned that song. She and Eve used to sing it together. I relaxed and let her cradle me. "Hello, little Enzo, so glad to see you, too. . . ."

I would like to tell you that I am such a master of my destiny that I contrived the entire situation, that I made myself crazy so Zoë could calm me on this trip, and thus, would be distracted from her own pain and agitation. Truth be told, however, I have to admit I was glad she was holding me; I was very afraid, and I was grateful for her care.

The line of cars trudged steadily but slowly. Many cars were stopped on the side of the road to wait out the storm. The weather men and women on the radio said waiting would be worse, however, as the weather front was stalled, the ceiling was low, and when the warm air arrived as anticipated, the ice would turn to rain and the flooding would begin.

When we reached the turnoff for Highway 2, there was an announcement on the radio that Blewett Pass was closed because of a jackknifed tractor-trailer rig. We would have to make a long detour to reach I-90 near George, Washington. Denny anticipated faster travel on I-90 because of its size, but it was worse, not better. The rains had begun and the median was more like a spill-way than a grassy divide between east and west. Still, we continued our journey because there was little else we could do.

After seven hours of grueling travel and still two hours away from Seattle in good driving weather, we stopped at a McDonald's and Denny purchased food for us to eat—I got chicken nuggets—then we pressed onward to Easton.

Outside Easton, where snow was piled on the sides of the highway, Denny stopped his car alongside dozens of other cars and trucks in the chain-up area and ventured into the freezing rain. He lay down on the pavement and installed the tire chains, which took half of an hour, and when he climbed back into the car, he was soaking wet and shivering.

"They're going to close the pass soon," Denny said to

me and Zoë. "That trucker heard it on the radio."

It was nasty and horrible, snow and ice and freezing rain, but we pushed on, our little old BMW chugging up the mountain until we reached the summit where they have the ski lifts, and then everything changed. There was no snow, no ice, just rain. We rejoiced in the rain!

Shortly, Denny stopped the car to remove the chains, which took another half hour and got him soaking again, and then we were going downhill. The windshield wipers flipped back and forth as quickly as they could, but they didn't help much. The visibility was terrible. Denny held the wheel tightly and squinted into the darkness, and we eventually reached North Bend and then Issaquah and then the floating bridge across Lake Washington. It was near midnight—the five-hour drive having taken more than ten—when we finally pulled into our driveway at home.

Denny carried Zoë to her room and put her to sleep. He turned on the television and we watched news reports of Snoqualmie Pass—where we had just been!—being shut down because of a rock slide that had destroyed the westbound lanes. Denny went into the bathroom and shed his wet clothes; he returned wearing sweat pants and an old T-shirt. He pulled a beer from the refrigerator and opened it. He took out his cell phone and pressed a button.

"Maxwell," Denny said after a moment. "I assume Eve is asleep?"

He paused.

"Tell her we're fine. We're back home. She should call first thing in the morning."

There was a great deal of shouting I could hear on the other end of the phone, but I couldn't make out the words. Denny let the shouting go on for quite some time before he said, "Maxwell, I am far too exhausted for this right now. Yell at me tomorrow."

He hung up the phone, and when it buzzed again, he refused to answer. It buzzed again and again, relentlessly. And when his landline rang, he refused that, too.

He didn't even get under the covers. He lay back on the bed, his knees hanging over the end and his feet dangling to the floor, and he fell into a fast, long sleep and didn't wake up until morning.

twenty-five

That year we had a cold spell in each winter month. Then when the first warm day of spring finally arrived in April, the trees and flowers and grasses burst to life with such intensity that the television news had to proclaim an allergy emergency. The drugstores literally ran out of allergy medicine. But while the rest of the world was focused on the inconvenience of hay fever, the people in my world had other things to do. Eve continued with the unstoppable process of dying. Zoë spent too much time with her grandparents, and Denny and I worked at trying to ease the pain we felt in our hearts.

Still, Denny allowed for an occasional diversion, and that April, one presented itself. He had gotten a job offer from one of the racing schools he worked for. They had been hired to provide race car drivers for a television commercial, and they asked Denny to be one of the drivers. The racecourse was in California, a place called Thunderhill Raceway Park. I knew it was happening in April because Denny talked about it quite a bit; he was very excited. But I had no idea that he planned to drive himself there, a ten-hour trip. And I had even less of an idea that he planned on taking me with him.

Oh, the joy! Denny and me and our BMW, driving all day and into the evening like a couple of banditos running from the law. Like partners in crime. It had to be a crime to lead such a life as we led, a life in which one could escape one's troubles by racing cars!

The drive down wasn't very special. The middle of Oregon is not noted for its scenic beauty, though other parts of Oregon are. And the mountain passes in northern California were still somewhat snowy, which made me nervous. Luckily, the snow of the Siskiyous was confined to the shoulders of the highway, and the road surface was bare and wet. And then we fell out of the sky and into the green fields north of Sacramento.

The track was relatively new and well cared for. It was challenging, with twists and elevation changes and so much to look at. The morning after we arrived, Denny took me jogging. We jogged the entire track. He was doing it to familiarize himself with the surface. You can't really see a track from inside a race car traveling at one hundred fifty miles per hour or more, he said. You have to get out and *feel* it.

Denny explained to me what he was looking for. Bumps in the pavement that might upset one's suspension. He touched the pavement at the midpoint of the turns and felt the condition of the asphalt. Were the small stones worn smooth? Could he find better grip slightly off the established racing line? And there were tricks to the slope of certain turns, places where the track appeared level from inside a car but were actually graded ever so slightly to allow rainwater to run off the track and not puddle dangerously.

After we had traveled the entire track, we returned to the paddock—the infield of the track, where the cars get worked on. Two large trucks had arrived. Several men in racing-crew uniforms erected tents and canopies, and laid out an elaborate food service. Other men unloaded six beautifully identical Aston Martin DB5 automobiles, the kind made famous by James Bond. Denny introduced himself to a man who carried a clipboard and walked with the gait of someone in charge. His name was Ken.

"Thanks for your dedication," Ken said, "but you're early."

"I wanted to walk the track," Denny explained.

"It's too early for race engines," he said, "but you can

take your street car out if you want. Just keep it sane."

"Thanks," Denny said, and he looked at me and winked.

We went over to a crew truck, and Denny caught the arm of a crew member.

"I'm Denny," he said. "One of the drivers."

The man shook his hand and introduced himself as Pat.

"I'm going to take my BMW out for a few easy laps. Ken said it was okay. I was wondering if you had a tie-down I could borrow."

"What do you need a tie-down for?" Pat asked.

Denny glanced at me quickly, and Pat laughed. "Hey, Jim," he called to another man. "This guy wants to borrow a tie-down so he can take his dog for a joyride."

They both laughed, and I was a little confused.

"I have something better," the Jim guy said. He went around to the cab of the truck and returned a minute later with a bedsheet.

Denny told me to get in the front seat of his car and sit, which I did. They wrapped the sheet over me, pressing me to the seat, leaving only my head sticking out. They somehow secured the sheet tightly from behind.

"Too tight?" Denny asked.

I was too excited to reply. He was going to take me out in his car!

"Take it easy on him until you see if he has a stomach for it," Pat said.

"You've done this before?" asked Denny.

"Oh, yeah," said Pat. "My dog used to love it."

Denny walked around to the driver's side. He took his helmet out of the backseat and squeezed it onto his head. He got into the car and put on his seat belt.

"One bark means 'slower,' two means 'faster,' got it?" I barked twice, and that surprised him and Pat and Jim, who were both leaning in the passenger window.

"He wants to go faster already," Jim said. "You've got yourself a good dog there."

The paddock at Thunderhill Raceway Park is tucked between two long parallel straights; the rest of the course fans out from the paddock area like butterfly wings. We cruised very slowly through the hot pit area and to the track entrance. "We're going to take it easy," Denny said, and off we went.

Being on a track was a new experience for me. No buildings, no signs, no sense of proportion. It was like running through a field, gliding over a plain. Denny shifted smoothly, but I noticed he drove more aggressively than he did on the street. He revved the car much higher, and his braking was much harder.

Around the turns we went. Down the straights we

picked up speed. We weren't going very fast, maybe sixty. But I really felt the speed around the turns, when the tires made a hollow, ghostly sound, almost like an owl. I felt special, being with Denny on the racetrack. He had never taken me on a track before. I felt sure and relaxed; being held firmly to the seat was comforting. The windows were open, and the wind was fresh and cold. I could have driven like that all day.

After three laps he looked over at me.

"You want to try a hot lap?"

A hot lap? I barked twice. Then I barked twice again. Denny laughed.

"Sing out if you don't like it," he said, "one long howl." He firmly pressed the accelerator to the floor.

There is nothing like it. The sensation of speed. Nothing in the world can compare.

"Hold on, now," Denny said, "we're taking this at speed."

Fast, we went, hurtling, faster. I watched the turn approach, scream at us until we were practically past it and then he was off the accelerator and hard on the brakes.

And then he cranked the wheel left and he was back on the gas and we were pushing through the turn. The force of gravity shoving us toward the outside of the car but the tires holding us in place. They were not hooting, those tires, no. The owl was dead. The tires were screeching, they were shouting, howling, crying in pain, *ahhhhh*!

He relaxed on the wheel at the midpoint and the car drifted toward the exit and he was full on the gas and we flew—*flew!*—out of that turn and toward the next and the next after that. Fifteen turns at Thunderhill. Fifteen. And I love them all equally. I adore them all. Each one is different, each with its own particular sensation, but each so magnificent! Around the track we went, faster and faster, lap after lap.

"You okay?" he asked, looking over at me as we sped at nearly one hundred twenty miles per hour.

I barked twice.

"I'm gonna use up my tires if you keep me out here," he said. "One more lap."

Yes, one more lap. I live my life for one more lap. I give my life for one more lap! Please, God, please give me one more lap!

And that lap was spectacular. I lifted my eyes as Denny instructed. "Big eyes, far eyes," he said to me. Those reference points he had identified when we walked the track moved by so quickly it took me some time to realize that he was not even seeing them. He was *living* them! He had programmed the map of the racecourse into his brain and it was there like a GPS navigational system; when we slowed for a turn, his head was up and looking at *the next turn*, not at the turn we were driving.

But his attention—and his *intention*—was far ahead, to the next turn and the one beyond that. With every breath he adjusted, he corrected, but he did it all instinctively; I saw, then, how in a race he could plot now to pass another driver three or four laps later. His thinking, his strategies, his mind; all of Denny unfolded for me that day.

After a cool-down lap, we pulled into the paddock, and the entire crew was waiting. They surrounded the car and their hands released me from my harness and I leapt to the ground.

"Did you like it?" one of them asked me, and I barked, *Yes!* I barked and jumped high in the air.

"You were really moving out there," Pat said to Denny. "We've got a real racer on the set."

"Well, Enzo barked twice," Denny explained with a laugh. "Two barks means 'faster!'"

They laughed, and I barked twice again. Faster! The feeling. The sensation. The movement. The speed. The car. The tires. The sound. The wind. The track surface. The exit. The shift point. The braking zone. The ride. It's all about the ride!

I floated through the rest of our trip. I dreamed of

going out again at speed, but I suspected that more track time for me was unlikely. Still. I had my memory, my experience I could relive in my mind again and again. Two barks means "faster." Sometimes, to this day, in my sleep I bark twice because I am dreaming of Denny driving me around Thunderhill, and I bark twice to say "faster." One more lap, Denny! *Faster!*

twenty-six

Six months came and six months left and Eve was still alive. Then seven months. Then eight. On the first of May, Denny and I were invited to the Twins' for dinner, which was unusual because it was a Monday night, and I never went with Denny on a weeknight visit. We stood awkwardly in the living room with the empty hospital bed while Trish and Maxwell prepared dinner. Eve was absent.

I wandered down the hallway to investigate, and I found Zoë playing quietly by herself in her room. Her room in Maxwell and Trish's house was much larger than her room at home, and it was filled with all the things a little girl could want. Lots of dolls and toys and frilly bed skirts and clouds painted on the ceiling. She was busy in her dollhouse and didn't notice me enter.

I spotted a sock ball on the floor and I pounced on it. I playfully dropped it at Zoë's feet, nudged it with my nose, and then dropped down to my elbows, leaving my haunches tall and my tail upright: universal sign language for "Let's play!" But she ignored me.

So I tried again. I snatched up the socks, flung them into the air, and batted them with my snout. Then retrieved them for myself, dropped them again at Zoë's feet, and faced downward. She pushed the socks aside with her foot.

I barked expectantly, one last attempt. She turned and looked at me seriously.

"That's a baby game," she said. "I have to be a grown-up now."

My little Zoë, a grown-up at her young age. A sad thought. Disappointed, I walked slowly to the door and looked back at her over my shoulder.

"Sometimes bad things happen," she said to herself. "Sometimes things change, and we have to change, too."

She was speaking someone else's words, and I'm not sure she believed them or even understood them.

I returned to the living room and waited with Denny until, finally, Eve emerged from the hallway where the bedroom and bathrooms were. The nurse was helping Eve walk. And Eve was brilliant. She was wearing a gorgeous dress, long and navy blue and cut just so. She wore the lovely string of small pearls from Japan that Denny had given her for their fifth anniversary. And someone had done her makeup and her hair, and she was beaming. Even though she needed help for her runway walk, she was walking the runway, and Denny gave her a standing ovation.

"Today is the first day I am not dead," Eve said to us. "And we're having a party."

To live every day as if it had been stolen from death, that is how I would like to live. To feel the joy of life, as Eve felt the joy of life. To say, "I am alive, I am wonderful, I am. I am." That is something to aspire to. When I am a person, that is how I will live my life.

The party was festive. Everyone was happy, and those who were not happy pretended that they were. Even Zoë came alive with her usual humor, apparently forgetting for a time her need to be a grown-up. When the hour came for us to leave, Denny kissed Eve deeply. "I love you so much," he said. "I wish you could come home."

"I want to come home," she replied. "I *will* come home."

She was tired, so she sat on the sofa and called me to her; I let her rub my ears. Denny was helping Zoë get ready for her bedtime. The Twins, for once, were keeping a respectful distance.

"I know Denny's disappointed," she said to me. "They're all disappointed. They want me to be cured of this cancer. And if I could just grab it and hold it in front of me, maybe I could be. But I can't hold it, Enzo. It's bigger than me. It's everywhere."

In the other room we could hear Zoë playing in the bath, Denny laughing with her, as if they had no worries in the world.

She shook her head to rid herself of her sad thoughts and looked down at me.

"Do you see?" she asked. "I'm not afraid of it anymore. I wanted you with me before because I wanted you to protect me, but I'm not afraid of it anymore. Because it's not the end."

She laughed the Eve laugh that I remembered.

"But you knew that," she said. "You know everything."

We took our leave, Denny and I. I didn't sleep in the car on the ride home as I usually did. I watched the bright lights of Bellevue and Medina flicker by, so beautiful. Crossing the lake on the floating bridge, I saw the glow of Madison Park and Leschi, the buildings of downtown peeking out from behind the Mount Baker ridge, the city sharp and crisp, all the dirt and age hidden by the night.

She died that night. Her last breath took her soul; I saw it in my dream. I saw her soul leave her body as she breathed out and then she had no more needs. She was released from her body and, being released, she continued her journey elsewhere. High in the heavens where soul material gathers and plays out all our dreams and joys.

twenty-seven

In the morning, Denny didn't know about Eve, and I, having awakened in a fog from my dream, barely suspected. He drove me over to Luther Burbank Park on the eastern shore of Mercer Island. Since it was a warm spring day, it was a good choice of dog parks, as it afforded lake access so that Denny could throw the ball and I could swim after it. The park was empty of other dogs; we were by ourselves.

"We'll move her back home," Denny said to me as he threw the ball. "And Zoë. We should all be together. I miss them."

I swam out into the cold lake and retrieved the ball.

"This week," he said. "This week I'll bring both of them home."

And he threw the ball again. I waded over the rocky bottom until my body floated and then I paddled out to the ball. I bobbed for it in the lake, and returned. When I dropped the ball at Denny's feet and looked up, I saw that he was on his cell phone. After a moment he nodded and hung up.

"She's gone," he said, and then he sobbed loudly and turned away, crying into the crook of his arm so I couldn't see.

I am not a dog who runs away from things. I had never run away from Denny before that moment, and I have never run away since. But in that moment, I had to run. I burst off down the short path and out onto the big field. Over the asphalt path and down the other side, where I found what I was looking for: untamed wilderness. I needed to go wilding. I was upset, sad, angry— something! I needed to do something! So I ran.

The twigs and vines whipped my face. The rough earth hurt my feet. But I ran until I could run no more. I had to do it. I missed Eve so much I couldn't be a human anymore and feel the pain that humans feel. I had to be an animal again. My trying to live to human standards had done nothing for Eve; I ran until my paws were scratched and sore and my fur was filthy with mud and leaves and burrs. I ran for Eve.

I slept in the bushes. Sometime later I emerged, myself again. Denny found me and he said nothing. He led me to the car. I got in the backseat and fell asleep again immediately. And while I slept I dreamed of Eve.

twenty-eight

For Eve, her death was the end of a painful battle. For Denny it was the beginning.

What I did in the park was selfish because it was about satisfying my basest needs. It was also selfish because it prevented Denny from going to Zoë right away. He was angry with me for having delayed him in the park. But to postpone, even for a short time, what he was to find at the home of the Twins might have been the most merciful thing I could have done for him.

When I awoke from my slumber, we were at Maxwell and Trish's house. In the driveway was a windowless white van. Denny parked in such a way as to not block the vehicle, and then he led me around the side of the house to the hose in back. He turned on the hose and rinsed the dirt from me in a rough and joyless manner; it was not a bath, it was a scrubbing.

"What did you get into out there?" he asked me.

When I was clean, he released me and I shook myself dry. He went to the French doors on the patio and knocked. After a moment, Trish appeared. She opened the door and embraced Denny. She was crying.

After a long time, during which Maxwell and Zoë also appeared, Denny ended the embrace and asked, "Where is she?"

Trish pointed. "We told them to wait for you," she said. Denny stepped into the house, touching Zoë's head as he passed. After he disappeared, Trish looked at Maxwell.

"Let him have a minute," she said.

And they, with Zoë, stepped outside and closed the French door so that Denny could be alone with Eve for the last time, even though she was no longer living.

I waited with them until Denny returned. When he did, he went to Zoë immediately, picked her up, and held her tightly. She squeezed his neck.

"I'm so sad," he said.

"Me, too," said Zoë.

He sat on one of the teak deck chairs with her on his knee. She buried her face in his shoulder and stayed like that.

"The people from the funeral home will take her now,"

Trish said. "We'll bury her with our family. It's what she wanted."

"I know," he said, nodding. "When?"

"Before the end of the week," she replied.

"What can I do?" asked Denny.

Trish looked at Maxwell. "We'll take care of the arrangements," Maxwell said. "But we did want to speak with you about something."

Denny waited for Maxwell to continue, but he didn't.

"You haven't eaten breakfast, Zoë," Trish said. "Come with me and I'll fix you an egg."

Zoë obediently followed Trish into the house.

When she was gone, Denny leaned back with his eyes closed and sighed heavily, his face lifted to the sky. He stayed like that for a long time. Minutes. He was a statue. While Denny was immobile, Maxwell shifted his weight from one foot to the other and back. Several times Maxwell began speaking but stopped himself. He seemed somehow reluctant.

"I knew it was coming," Denny said, finally, his eyes still closed. "But still . . . I'm surprised."

Maxwell nodded to himself. "That's what concerns Trish and me," he said.

Denny opened his eyes and looked at Maxwell. "Concerns you?" he asked, taken aback.

"That you haven't made preparations."

"Preparations?"

"You have no plan."

"Plan?"

"You keep repeating the last thing I've said," Maxwell observed after a pause.

"Because I don't understand what you're talking about," Denny said.

"That's what concerns us."

Denny, still sitting, leaned forward and screwed up his face at Maxwell.

"What exactly are you concerned about, Maxwell?" he asked.

Then Trish was there. "Zoë is eating an egg and toast, and watching TV in the kitchen," she announced. She looked at Maxwell expectantly.

"We've just started," Maxwell said.

"Oh," Trish said, "I thought . . . What have you said so far?"

"Why don't you take it from the top, Trish," Denny said. "Maxwell is having some difficulty with the opening. You're concerned. . . ."

Trish glanced around, apparently disappointed that their concerns hadn't already been resolved.

"Well," she began, "Eve's passing is obviously a terrible

tragedy. Still, we've been anticipating it for many months. Maxwell and I have discussed at great length our lives— the lives of all of us—in the aftermath of Eve's death. We discussed it with Eve, as well, just so you know. And we believe that the best situation for all parties involved would be for us to have custody of Zoë. To raise her in a warm and stable family situation, to provide her with the kind of privileges we can offer her. We think it will be best. We hope you understand that this is in no way a judgment of you as a person or your fathering abilities. It is simply what is in Zoë's best interest."

Denny looked from one of them to the other, a confused look still on his face, but he said nothing.

I was confused, too. It was my understanding that Denny had allowed Eve to live with the Twins so they could spend time with their dying daughter, and that he had allowed Zoë to live with the Twins so she could spend time with her dying mother. As I understood it, once Eve died, Zoë would be with us. The idea of a transition period made some sense to me. Eve had died the previous night; for Zoë to spend the following day—or even a few days— with her grandparents made sense. But, custody? Have Zoë live with them all the time?

"What do you think?" Trish asked.

"You can't have custody of Zoë," Denny said simply.

Maxwell sucked in his cheeks, crossed his arms, and tapped his fingers against his biceps, which were clad in a dark polyester knit.

"I know this is hard for you," Trish said. "But you have to agree that we have the advantages of parental experience. We have available free time. And money that will ensure Zoë's education through whatever level she might choose to pursue. We also have a large home in a safe neighborhood that has many young families and many children her age."

Denny thought for a moment. "You can't have custody of Zoë," he said.

"I told you," Maxwell said to Trish.

"If you could just sleep on it," Trish said to Denny. "I'm sure you will see that what we're doing is right. It's best for all. You can pursue your racing career and Zoë can grow up in a loving and supportive environment. It's what Eve wanted."

"How do you know that?" Denny asked quickly. "She told you?"

"She did."

"But she didn't tell me," said Denny.

"I don't know why she wouldn't have," Trish said.

"She didn't," Denny said firmly.

Trish forced a smile. "Will you sleep on it?" she asked.

"Will you think about what we've said? It will be much easier."

"No, I will not sleep on it," Denny said, rising from the chair. "You can't have custody of my daughter. Final answer."

The Twins sighed simultaneously. Trish shook her head in dismay. Maxwell reached into his back pocket and removed a business envelope. "We didn't want it to have to be this way," he said, and he handed the envelope to Denny.

"What's this?" Denny asked.

"Open it," Maxwell said.

Denny opened the envelope and removed several sheets of paper. He glanced at them briefly.

"What does this mean?" he asked.

"I don't know if you have a lawyer," Maxwell said. "But if you don't, you should get one. We're suing for custody of our granddaughter."

Denny flinched like he had been punched in the gut. He fell back into the deck chair, his hands still clinging to the documents.

"I finished my egg," Zoë announced. None of us had noticed her return, but there she was. She climbed onto Denny's lap. "Are *you* hungry?" she asked. "Grandma can make you an egg, too."

"No," he said apologetically. "I'm not hungry."

She thought a moment. "Are you still sad?" she asked.

"Yes," he said after a pause. "I'm still very sad."

"Me, too," she agreed, and she laid her head on his chest. Denny looked at the Twins. Maxwell's long arm hung on Trish's narrow shoulders like some kind of heavy chain. And then I saw something change in Denny. I saw his face tighten with resolve.

"Zoë," he said, standing her up. "You run inside and pack your things, okay?"

"Where are we going?" she asked.

"We're going home now." Zoë smiled and started off, but Maxwell stepped forward.

"Zoë, stop right there," he said. "Daddy has some errands he has to run. You'll stay with us for now."

"How dare you!" Denny said. "Who do you think you are?"

"I'm the one who's been raising her for the past eight months," Maxwell said, his jaw set. Zoë looked from her father to her grandfather. She didn't know what to do. No one knew what to do. It was a standoff. And then Trish stepped in.

"Run inside and put your dolls together," she said to Zoë, "while we talk a little more."

Zoë reluctantly withdrew.

"Let her stay with us, Denny," Trish pleaded. "We can work this out. I know we can work it out. Let her stay with us while the lawyers come up with some kind of compromise. You were fine with her staying here before."

"You begged me to let her stay here," Denny said to her.

"I'm sure we can work this out."

"No, Trish," he said. "I'm taking her home with me."

"And who's going to take care of her when you're at work?" Maxwell snapped, shaking with anger. "When you're off at your races for days at a time? Who will take care of her if, God forbid, she were to get sick? Or would you just ignore it, hide it from the doctors until she was on the verge of death, like you did with Eve?"

"I didn't hide Eve from the doctors."

"And yet she never saw anyone—"

"She refused!" Denny cried out. "She refused to see anyone!"

"You could have forced her," Maxwell shouted.

"No one could force Eve to do anything Eve didn't want to do," Denny said. "*I* certainly couldn't."

Maxwell clenched his fists tightly. The tendons in his neck bulged. "And that's why she's dead," he said.

"What?" Denny asked incredulously. "This is a joke! I'm not continuing this conversation." He glared at

Maxwell and started toward the house.

"I regret the day she met you," Maxwell muttered after him.

Denny stopped at the door and called inside. "Zoë, let's go now. We can stop by later to get your dolls."

Zoë emerged looking confused, holding an armful of stuffed animals. "Can I take these?" she asked.

"Yes, honey. But let's go now. We'll come back later for the rest." Denny ushered her toward the path that led around to the front of the house.

"You're going to regret this," Maxwell hissed at Denny as he passed. "You have no idea what you're getting yourself into."

"Let's go, Enzo," Denny said.

We walked around to the driveway and got into our car. Maxwell followed us and watched Denny strap Zoë into her car seat. Denny started the engine.

"You're going to regret this," Maxwell said again. "Mark my words."

Denny pulled the driver's-side door closed with a slam that shook the car. "Do I have a lawyer?" he said to himself. "I work at the most prestigious BMW and Mercedes service center in Seattle. Who does he think he's dealing with? I have a good relationship with all the best lawyers in this town. *And* I have their home phone numbers."

We pulled out of the driveway with a spray of gravel at Maxwell's feet, and as we took off up the idyllic, twisty Mercer Island road, I couldn't help but notice that the white van was gone. And with it, Eve.

twenty-nine

With experience, a driver adjusts his understanding of how a car feels when it is near its limits. A driver becomes comfortable driving on the edge, so when his tires begin to slip, he can easily correct, pause, and recover. Knowing where and when he can push for a little extra becomes ingrained in his being.

When the pressure is intense and the race is only half completed, a driver who is being chased relentlessly by a competitor realizes that he might be better off pushing from behind than pulling from the front. In that case, the smart move is to yield his lead to the trailing car and let the other driver pass. Our driver can then tuck in behind and make the new leader "drive his mirrors"—worry about the car behind him.

Sometimes, however, it is important to hold one's

position and not allow the pass. For strategic reasons, psychological reasons. Sometimes a driver simply has to prove that he is better than his competition.

Racing is about discipline and intelligence, not about who has the heavier foot. The one who drives smart will always win in the end.

thirty

Zoë insisted on going to school the next day, and when Denny said he would pick her up at dismissal time, she complained that she wanted to play with her friends in the after-school program. Denny reluctantly agreed.

"I'll pick you up a little earlier than I usually do," he said when we dropped her off. He must have been afraid that the Twins would try to steal her away.

From Zoë's school, we drove up Union to Fifteenth Avenue and found a parking spot directly across from Victrola Coffee. Denny tied my leash to a bicycle stand and went inside; he returned a few minutes later with coffee and a scone. He untied me and told me to sit underneath an outdoor table, which I did. A quarter of an hour later, we were joined by someone else. A large but compact man composed of circles: round head, round torso, round thighs, round hands. There was no hair on the top of his head, but a lot on the sides. He was wearing very wide jeans and a large gray sweatshirt with a giant purple W on it.

"Good morning, Dennis," the man said. "Please accept my sincere condolences for your devastating loss." The man then wedged himself between the metal arms of the other sidewalk chair by our table. He was not fat, and in fact, he might have been considered muscular in some circles, yet he was very large.

"Good-looking dog," he said. "He has some terrier in him?"

I lifted my head. Me?

"I don't know exactly," Denny said. "Probably."

"Good-looking animal," the man mused. I was impressed that he noticed me at all.

"Let's get down to business," the man said. "This consultation will cost you an oil change. My Mercedes is very thirsty. An oil change, whether or not you decide to retain me."

"Fine," said Denny.

"Let me see the paperwork," replied the man. Denny handed him the envelope Maxwell had given him. The man took it and removed the papers.

"They said Eve told them she wanted Zoë to be raised by them," said Denny.

"I don't care about that," the man said.

"Sometimes she was on so many drugs, she would have said anything," Denny said desperately. "She may have said it, but she couldn't have *meant* it."

"I don't care what anyone said or why they said it," the man said sharply. "Children are not possessions. They cannot be given away or traded in the marketplace. Everything that happens will be done in the best interest of the child."

"That's what they said," Denny said. "Zoë's best interest."

"They're educated," the man said. "Still, the mother's final wishes are irrelevant. How long were you married?"

"Six years," replied Denny.

"Any other children?"

"No."

The man drank his latte and leafed through the papers. He was a curious man, full of twitches and extra movements. It took me several minutes to realize that when he touched his hand to his hip pocket, it was because he had some kind of buzzing device hidden away. By touching it he could stop its buzzing. This man's attention was in many places at once. And yet, when he locked eyes with Denny, I could sense the totality of his focus. Denny could, too, I knew, because in those moments, Denny's tension slackened noticeably.

"Are you in a drug treatment program?" the man asked.

"No."

"Have you ever been convicted of a felony? Spent any time in jail?"

"No."

The man stuffed the papers back in the envelope. "This is nothing," he said. "Where is your daughter now?"

"She wanted to go to school. Should I have kept her home?"

"No, that's good. You're being responsive to her needs. That's important. Listen, this is not something you should be overly concerned with. I'll ask for a ruling by the court. The child will be yours free and clear."

"Okay," Denny said.

"Don't panic. Don't get mad. Be polite. Call them and give them my information. Tell them all correspondence has to be directed to me as your attorney. I'll call their lawyers and let them know the big dog—that's me—is in your corner. My feeling is they're looking for a soft spot; they're hoping you'll go away quietly. Grandparents are like that. Grandparents are convinced they're better parents than their own kids, whose lives they've already messed up. The problem is, grandparents are pains in the butt because they have money. Do they have money?"

"Plenty."

"And you?"

"Oil changes for life," Denny said with a forced smile.

"Oil changes ain't going to cut it, Dennis. My rate is four hundred fifty dollars an hour. I need a twenty-five-hundred-dollar retainer. Do you have it?"

"I'll get it, Mark," Denny said.

Mark sucked in his cheeks and nodded. "Me to you, Dennis? We're talking about seven or eight grand to make this thing go away. You can do that, right? Of course you can. I waive my retainer for you, my friend." He stood up and the chair almost stood with him, but he shucked himself out of it before it embarrassed him in front of the Victrola crowd. "This is a totally bogus custody suit. I can't even imagine why they would bother to file it. Call the in-laws and tell them everything goes through me. I'll have my assistant on this today. They're playing you for a sucker, and you aren't a sucker, are you, champ?"

He cuffed Denny on the chin. "Be cool with them," Mark said. "Don't get angry. Be cool, and everything is in little Zoë's best interest, got it? Always say everything is for her. Got it?"

"Got it," Denny said.

The man paused solemnly. "How are you holding up, friend?"

"I'm fine," Denny said.

"Ah. You're a good man, Dennis," Mark said. "I'll take care of this. Of all the things you have to worry about, this is not one of them. You let *me* worry about this part. You take care of your daughter, okay?"

"Thanks," replied Denny.

Mark trundled off down the street, and when he had rounded the corner, Denny looked at me and held his hands out in front of himself. They were shaking. He didn't say anything, but he looked at his hands trembling and then he looked at me. I knew what he was thinking. He was thinking that if he just had a steering wheel to hold on to, his hands wouldn't shake. If he had a steering wheel to hold on to, everything would be all right.

thirty-one

I spent most of the day hanging out in the garage with the guys who fix the cars because the owners of the shop didn't like it when I was in the lobby where the customers could see me.

I felt strangely anxious that day, in a very human way. People are always worried about what's happening next. On a normal dog day, I can sit still for hours on end with no effort. But that day I was anxious. I was nervous and worried, uneasy and distracted. I paced around and never felt settled. I didn't care for the sensation, yet I realized it was possibly a natural progression of my evolving soul, and therefore I tried my best to embrace it.

One of the garage bays was open, and a sticky drizzle fogged the air. Skip, the big funny man with the long beard, dutifully washed the cars that were ready for pickup, even though it was raining.

"Rain isn't dirty, *dirt* is dirty," he repeated to himself, a Seattle car-washing mantra. He squeezed his clump of sponge, and soapy water rushed like a river down the windshield of an immaculately cared-for British racing green BMW 2002. I lay, head between my forelegs, just inside the threshold of the garage, watching him work.

The day seemed like it would never end, until the Seattle police car showed up and two policemen got out and walked to the lobby door and went inside.

I nosed through the swinging door in the garage bay and into the file room. I wandered up behind the counter, which Mike was attending. "Afternoon, officers," I heard Mike say. "A problem with your car?"

"Are you Dennis Swift?" one of them asked.

"I am not," Mike replied.

"Is he here?"

Mike hesitated. I could smell his sudden tension. "He may have left for the day," Mike said. "Let me check. Can I tell him who's calling?"

"We have a warrant for his arrest," one of the policemen said.

"I'll see if he's still in the back."

Mike turned and stumbled into me. "Enzo. Clear out, boy." I followed him into the back, where Denny was at the computer, logging invoices for the people who wanted their cars by the end of the day.

"Den," Mike said. "There are a couple of cops out front with a warrant."

"For?" Denny asked, not even looking up from the screen, tap-tap-tapping away at his invoices.

"You. For your arrest."

Denny stopped what he was doing. "For what?" he asked.

"I didn't get the details. But they're in uniform and I don't think it's a prank."

Denny stood up and started for the lobby.

"I told them you might have left for the day," Mike said, indicating the back door with his chin.

"I appreciate the thought, Mike. But if they've got a warrant, they probably know where I live. Let me find out what this is all about."

Like a train, the three of us snaked through the file room and up to the counter. "I'm Denny Swift."

The police nodded. "Could you step out from behind the counter, sir?" one of them asked.

"Is there a problem? Can you tell me what this is all about?" There were half a dozen people sitting in the lobby waiting for their invoices to be prepared; they all looked up from their reading material.

"Please step out from behind the counter," the policeman said.

Denny hesitated for a moment, and then followed his instructions.

"We have a warrant for your arrest," one of the men said.

"For what?" Denny asked. "Can I see it? There must be some mistake."

The cop handed Denny a sheaf of paper. Denny read it. "You're joking," he said.

"No, sir," the cop said, taking back the papers. "Please place your hands on the counter and spread your legs."

Denny's boss, Craig, came out of the back.

"Officers?" he said, approaching them. "I don't believe this is necessary, and if it is, you can do it outside."

"Sir, hold!" the policeman said sternly, pointing a long finger at Craig.

But Craig was right. People were there, waiting for their BMWs and Mercedes gull-wings and other fancy cars. The police didn't have to do what they did in front of those people. They were customers. They trusted Denny, and now he was a criminal? What the police were doing wasn't right. There must have been a better way. But they had guns and batons. They had pepper spray and Tasers.

Denny followed their instructions and placed his hands on the counter and spread his legs; the cop patted him down thoroughly.

"Please turn around and place your hands behind your back," the cop said.

"You don't need handcuffs," Craig said angrily. "He's not running anywhere!"

"Sir!" the cop barked. "Hold!"

Denny turned around and placed his hands behind his back. The officer cuffed him. "You have the right to remain silent," the cop said. "Anything you say can and will be held against you—"

"How long is this going to take?" Denny asked. "I have to pick up my daughter."

"That won't be necessary," the other police officer said.

"I can pick her up, Denny," Mike said.

"Your daughter is in protective custody," said the policeman.

"What?" shouted Denny, his confusion turning to fear. "Where is my daughter?"

". . . an attorney will be appointed to you . . ."

"Where is my daughter?"

"Who should I call?" asked Mike.

"Call Mark Fein," Denny said, desperate. "He's in the computer."

"Do you understand these rights as I have read them to you?" continued the policeman.

"Do you need me to bail you out?" Craig asked. "Whatever you need—"

"I have no idea what I need," Denny said. "Call Mark. He'll know what to do."

"*Do you understand the rights as I have read them?*" repeated the cop.

"I understand!" Denny snapped. "Yes. I understand!"

"What are you being arrested for?" Mike asked.

Denny looked to the officers, but they said nothing. They waited for Denny to answer the question. They were well trained in the sophisticated methods of breaking down a subject—make him voice his own crime.

"'Criminal negligence toward a child,'" Denny said.

"Abandonment," one of the cops clarified.

"But I didn't abandon anyone," Denny said to the cop. "Who's behind this? What child?"

There was a long pause. The people in the lobby were rapt. Denny was standing before them all, his hands bound behind his back. They could all see how he was a prisoner now, he had no use of his hands now, he could not race a car now. All attention was on the police and their black guns, sticks, and wands. It was true drama. Everyone wanted to know the answer to the question. *What child?*

"Your daughter," the cop replied simply. Without another word, the police took Denny away.

thirty-two

Much of what happened to Denny regarding the custody suit concerning Zoë as well as the charge of criminal neglect was not witnessed by me. These events spanned close to three years of our lives. One of the tactics of Maxwell and Trish was to drag out the process in order to deplete Denny of money and destroy his will. It was also intended to play off of his desire to see Zoë mature in a loving and supportive environment. I was denied access to much information. I was not invited to attend any of the legal proceedings, for instance. I was allowed to attend only a few of the meetings Denny had with his attorney, Mark Fein, specifically, those that occurred at Victrola Coffee. I did not accompany Denny to the police station after his arrest. I was not present for his booking, his arraignment, or his subsequent lie detector testing.

Much of what I will tell you about the ordeal that followed Eve's death is a reconstruction based on information compiled by me from secondhand knowledge, overheard conversations, and established legal practices as I have learned them from various television shows, most especially the *Law & Order* series and its spin-offs.

My intent, here, is to tell our story in a dramatically truthful way. While the facts may be less than accurate, please understand that the emotion is true. The intent is true.

thirty-three

They took Denny to a small room with a large table and many chairs. The walls had windows that looked out to the surrounding office, which was filled with police detectives doing their police work. Wooden blinds filtered the blue light that crept into the room, rippling the table and floor with long shadows.

No one bothered him. After being booked and fingerprinted and photographed, he was put in the room, alone, and left there, as if the police had forgotten him entirely. He sat by himself. He sat for hours with nothing. No coffee, no water, no restrooms, no radio. No distractions. Alone.

Did he despair? Did he silently scold himself for allowing himself to be in that situation? Or did he finally realize what it is like to be me, to be a dog? Did he understand, as those slow minutes ticked by, that being alone is not the same as being lonely? I like to think that he was alone for that time, but that he wasn't lonely. I like to think that he thought about his condition, but he did not despair.

And then the lawyer Mark Fein burst into the East Precinct on Seattle's Capitol Hill; he burst in and began shouting. That is Mark Fein's blustery style. Bellowing. Boisterous. Bold. Mark Fein is a capital letter B. He is shaped like the letter, and he acts like the letter. Brash. Brazen. Bullish. He blew down the door, bull-rushed the desk, blasted the sergeant on duty, and bailed out Denny.

"What the heck is this all about, Dennis?" Mark demanded on the street corner.

"It's nothing," Denny said, uninterested in the conversation.

"A charge of criminal neglect, Dennis! That's not nothing!"

"It's a lie," said Denny.

"Is it? Did you leave Zoë to wander off alone?"

"No."

"This is ridiculous," Mark said. "I can't believe the district attorney would sign off on these trumped-up charges! You can't arrest someone for abandonment because he dropped his daughter off at school. Your in-laws must have powerful friends."

Denny said nothing.

"I can get these charges dropped," Mark went on. "But the custody suit and the temporary restraining order is still very dangerous."

Denny ground his teeth; his jaw muscles bulged.

"My office, eight thirty tomorrow morning," Mark said. "Don't be late."

Denny burned.

"Where's Zoë?" he demanded. Mark Fein dug his heel into the pavement.

"They got to her before I could," he said. "The timing on this was not an accident."

"I'm going to get her," Denny said.

"Don't!" Mark snapped. "Let them be. Now is not the time for heroics. When you're stuck in quicksand, the worst thing you can do is struggle."

"So now I'm stuck in quicksand?" Denny asked.

"Dennis, you are in the quickest of all possible sand right now."

Denny wheeled around and started off.

"And don't leave the state," Mark called after him. But Denny had already rounded the corner and was gone.

thirty-four

Hands are the windows to a man's soul.

Watch in-car videos of race drivers enough, and you'll see the truth of this statement. The rigid, tense grip of one driver reflects his rigid, tense driving style. The nervous hand-shuffle of another driver proves how uncomfortable he is in the car. A driver's hands should be relaxed, sensitive, aware.

Seeing Denny's hands shake was as upsetting for me as it was for him. After Eve's death, he glanced at his hands often, held them before his eyes as if they weren't really his hands at all. He held them up and watched them shake. He tried to do it so no one would see. "Nerves," he would say to me whenever he caught me watching. "Stress." And then he would tuck them into his pants pockets and keep them there, out of sight.

When Mike and Tony brought me home later that night, Denny was waiting on the dark porch with his hands in his pockets. "Not only do I not want to talk about it," he said to them, "Mark told me not to. So."

They stood on the walk, looking up at him.

"Can we come in?" Mike asked.

"No," Denny replied, and then, aware of his abruptness, attempted to explain. "I don't feel like company right now."

They stared at him for a moment.

"You don't have to talk about what's going on," Mike said. "But it's good to *talk*. You can't keep everything inside. It's not healthy."

"You're probably right," Denny said. "But it's not how I operate. I just need to . . . process . . . what's going on, and then I'll be able to talk. But not now."

Neither Mike nor Tony moved. They looked at each other, and I could smell their anxiety. I wished that Denny would understand the depth of their concern for him. "You'll be all right?" Mike asked. "We don't have to worry about you doing something foolish?"

"I'll be all right," Denny said.

"You want us to keep Enzo or anything?" Mike asked.

"No."

"Bring you some groceries?"

Denny shook his head.

"He'll be all right," Tony said, and tugged at Mike's arm.

"My phone's always on," Mike said. "Twenty-four-hour crisis hotline. Need to talk, need anything, call me."

They retreated down the walk. "We fed Enzo!" Mike called from the alley. They left, and Denny and I went inside. He took his hands from his pockets and held them up to look at them shaking.

"Neglectful fathers don't get custody of their little girls," he said. "See how that works?"

I followed him into the kitchen and he went to the cupboard and took out a glass. Then he reached into where he kept the liquor and took out a bottle. He poured a drink. It was absurd. Depressed, stressed, hands shaking, and now he was going to get himself drunk? I couldn't stand for it. I barked sharply at him. He looked down at me, drink in hand, and I up at him. If I'd had hands, I would have opened one of them and slapped him with it.

"What's the matter, Enzo, too pathetic for you?"

I barked again.

"Don't judge me," he said. "That's not your job. Your job is to support me, not judge me."

He drank the drink and then glared at me, and I did judge him. He was acting just as they wanted him to act.

They were rattling him, and he was about to quit, and then it would be over. Then I'd have to spend the rest of my life with a drunkard. This wasn't my Denny. This was a pathetic character from a lousy television drama. And I didn't like him at all.

I left the room thinking I would go to bed, but I didn't want to sleep in the same room as this Denny impostor. This fake Denny. I went into Zoë's bedroom, curled up on the floor next to her bed, and tried to sleep. Zoë was the only one I had left.

Later—though I don't know how much—he stood in the doorway. "The first time I took you for a drive in my car when you were a puppy, you puked all over the seat," he said to me. "But I didn't give up on you." I lifted my head from the ground, not understanding his point.

"I put the booze away," he said. "I'm better than that."

He turned and walked away. I heard him shuffle around in the living room and then turn on the TV. So he didn't fall hopelessly into the bottle, the refuge of the weak and the sad. He got my point. Gestures are all that I have.

I found him on the couch watching a video of Eve, Zoë, and me. It was from years ago when we went to Long Beach, on the Washington coast. Zoë was a toddler. I remembered that weekend well; we were all so young, it seemed, chasing kites on the wide beach that went on for miles. I sat next to the couch and watched, too. We were so naive; we had no knowledge of where the road would take us, no idea that we would ever be separated.

"No race has ever been won in the first turn," he said. "But plenty of races have been lost there."

I looked at him. He reached out, settled his hand on the crown of my head, and scratched my ear like he has always done.

Yes: the race is long—to finish first, first you must finish.

thirty-five

I love very few things more than a nice long walk in the drizzle of Seattle. I don't care for the heaviness of real rain; I like the misting, the feeling of the tiny droplets on my muzzle and eyelashes. While rain is heavy and can suppress the scents, a light shower actually amplifies smells; it brings odor to life, and then carries it through the air to my nose. Which is why I love Seattle more than any other place, even Thunderhill Raceway Park. Because once the damp season begins, nary a day goes by without a helping of my much-loved drizzle.

Denny took me for a walk in the drizzle, and I loved it. Denny seemed to crave the change, too; instead of jeans, a sweatshirt, and his yellow slicker, he put on a pair of dark slacks. And he wore his black trench coat over a high-necked cashmere sweater.

We walked north out of Madison Valley and into the Arboretum. Once past the dangerous part, where there is no walkway, we turned off on the smaller road, and Denny released me from my leash.

This is what I love to do: I love to run through a field of wet grass that has not been mowed recently. I love to run, keeping my snout low to the ground so the grass and the sparkles of water cover my face. I imagine myself as a vacuum cleaner, sucking in all the smells, all the life, a spear of summer grass. It reminds me of my childhood, back on the farm in Spangle. There was no rain, but there was grass, there were fields, and I ran.

I ran and I ran that day. And Denny walked on, trudging steadily. At the point where we usually turned around, we kept going. We crossed the pedestrian bridge and curled up into Montlake. Denny reattached my leash and we crossed a larger road and we were in a new park! I loved this one, too. But it was different.

"Interlaken," Denny said to me as he unleashed me.

Interlaken. This park was not fields and flatland. It was a twisty ravine painted with vines and bushes and ground cover. Above, it was tented by the tallest of trees and a canopy of leaves. It was wonderful. As Denny followed the path, I bounded up and down the hillside, hiding in the low brush and pretending I was a secret agent. Or running as fast as I could through the obstacles and pretending I was a predator like in the movies. Hunting something down, tracking my prey.

For a long time we walked and ran in this park, me running five paces for every one of Denny's, until I was exhausted and thirsty. We emerged from the park and walked in a neighborhood that was new to me. Denny stopped in a café to purchase a cup of coffee for himself. He brought some water for me, which was in a paper cup and difficult to drink, but I managed.

And we continued walking.

I was getting quite tired. We had been out for more than two hours, but we kept walking. I recognized Fifteenth Avenue when we reached it, and I knew Volunteer Park quite well. But I was surprised when we went into Lake View Cemetery. I had never been there before. Following the paved road to the north, we looped around the central hill and came upon a temporary tent structure, under which many people were assembled.

They were all dressed nicely, and those who weren't protected from the drizzle by the tent were holding umbrellas. Immediately, I saw Zoë. Ah. Now I understood. Denny had dressed for Eve's burial. We approached the people, who were milling about, their attention fragmented. The proceedings had not yet begun.

We got very close to them, and then, suddenly, some-one broke off from the group. A man. And then another man, and another. The three of them walked toward us. One of them was Maxwell. The others were Eve's broth-ers, whose names I never knew because they showed themselves so infrequently.

"You're not welcome here," Maxwell said sternly.

"She's my wife," Denny said calmly. "The mother of my child."

She was there, the child. Zoë saw her father. She waved at him, and he waved back.

"You're not welcome here," Maxwell said again. "Leave, or I'll call the police. We have a restraining order."

"Why are you doing this?" asked Denny.

Maxwell pushed up into Denny's personal space. "You've never been good to Eve," Maxwell said. "And I will not trust you with Zoë."

"But I did nothing wrong—"

But Maxwell had already turned. "Please escort Mr. Swift away from here," he said to his two sons, and he abruptly walked away. In the distance, I saw Zoë, unable to contain herself any longer; she jumped out of her seat and ran toward us.

"Beat it," one of the men said.

"It's my wife's funeral," Denny said. "I'm staying."

Zoë reached us and leapt at Denny. He hoisted her into the air and propped her on his hip and kissed her cheek. "How's my baby?" he asked.

"How's my daddy?" she replied.

"I'm getting by," he said.

Trish rushed up to us. She inserted herself between Denny and the brothers. She told them to leave, and she turned to Denny.

"Please," she said. "I understand why you're here, but it can't be done like this. I really don't think you should stay." She hesitated for a moment, and then she said, "I'm sorry. You must be so alone."

Denny didn't respond. I looked up at him, and his eyes were full of tears. Zoë noticed, too, and started crying with him. "It's okay to cry," she said. "Grandma says crying helps because it washes away the hurting." He looked at Zoë for a long moment and she at him. Then he sighed sadly.

"You help Grandma and Grandpa be strong, okay?" he said. "I have some important business to take care of. About Mommy. There are things that have to be done."

"I know," she said.

"You'll stay with Grandma and Grandpa for a little

bit longer, until I get everything worked out, okay?"

"They told me I might stay with them for a while," said Zoë.

"Well," Denny said regretfully, "Grandma and Grandpa are very good at thinking ahead."

"We can all compromise," Trish said. "I know you're not a bad person—"

"There is no compromise," Denny said.

"Given time, you'll see. It's what's best for Zoë," replied Trish.

"Enzo!" Zoë called out suddenly, locating me beneath her. She squirmed loose of Denny and grabbed me around the neck. "Enzo!" I was surprised and pleased by her hearty greeting, so I licked her face.

Trish leaned in to Denny. "You must have been missing Eve terribly," she whispered to him.

"You can't begin to imagine," he said. Denny abruptly straightened and pulled away from her.

"Zoë," he said. "Enzo and I are going to watch from a special spot. Come on, Enzo." He bent down and kissed her forehead, and we walked away.

Zoë and Trish watched us go. We continued on the circular path and walked up the bump of a hill to the top. We stood underneath the trees, and, protected from the lightly falling rain, watched the whole thing. The people coming to attention. The man reading from a book. The people laying roses on the coffin. And everyone leaving in their cars.

When they were all gone, we walked down the hill and we stood before the mound of dirt and we cried. We kneeled and we cried and we grabbed at handfuls of the dirt, the mound, and we felt the last bit of her, the last part of her that we could feel, and we cried.

And finally, when we could do no more, we stood. And we began the long walk home.

thirty-six

The morning after Eve's burial, I could barely move. My body was so stiff, I couldn't even stand, and Denny had to look for me because I usually got up immediately and helped him with breakfast. I was eight years old, two years older than Zoë. While I was still too young to suffer an arthritic condition in my hips, that's exactly what I suffered from. It was an unpleasant condition, yes. But in a sense it was a relief that I could concentrate on my own difficulties rather than dwell on other things. Specifically, Zoë being stranded with the Twins.

The day after Eve's funeral, Denny took me to the vet. He was a thin man who smelled of hay, and who had a bottomless pocket full of treats. He felt my hips and I tried not to wince, but I couldn't help myself when he squeezed certain places. He diagnosed me, prescribed medication, and said there was nothing else he could do. Except, someday in the future, perform expensive surgery to replace my defective parts.

Denny thanked the man and drove me home.

"You have arthritis in your hips," he said to me.

If I'd had fingers, I'd have shoved them into my ears until I burst my own eardrums. Anything to avoid hearing.

"Arthritis," he repeated, shaking his head in amazement.

I shook my head, too. With my diagnosis, I knew, would come my end. Slowly, perhaps. Painfully, without a doubt; marked by the signposts laid out by the veterinarian. The visible becomes inevitable. The car goes where the eyes go. I thought of Eve and how quickly she embraced her death once the people around her agreed to it. I considered the foretelling of my own end and I tried to look away.

thirty-seven

The charges of criminal neglect were dropped, as Mark Fein had promised, but the temporary restraining order and the civil custody suit were still in place, which meant Denny didn't get to see Zoë at all for several months. Maxwell and Trish filed a motion to terminate Denny's right to custody of any kind, since he was clearly an unfit parent.

Well. We all play by the same rules. But some people spend more time reading those rules and figuring out how to make them work in their behalf.

I have seen movies that involve stolen children and the grief and terror that the parents feel when their children are taken by strangers. Denny felt every bit of that grief. And, in my own way, I did, too. And we knew where Zoë was. We knew who had taken her. And, still, we could do nothing.

Mark Fein suggested it would be a bad idea to tell Zoë about the legal proceedings. He suggested that Denny invent a story about driving race cars in Europe to explain his prolonged absence. Mark Fein also negotiated a letter exchange: notes and drawings made by Zoë would be delivered to Denny. And Denny could write letters to his child, as long as he agreed to allow those letters to be reviewed by the Twins before they were shown to Zoë. I will tell you, every vertical surface in our house was decorated with Zoë's delightful artwork.

As much as I wanted Denny to act, I respected his restraint. Denny has long admired the legendary driver Emerson Fittipaldi. "Emmo," as he was called, was a champion of great stature. Not only did Emmo never panic, Emmo never put himself in a position where he might have to. Like Emmo, Denny never took unnecessary risks.

While I, too, admire and try to emulate Emmo, I still think that I would like to drive like Ayrton Senna, full of emotion and daring. I would like to have driven by Zoë's school one day to pick her up unannounced, and then headed directly for Canada, where we could live by ourselves in peace for the rest of our lives.

But it was not my choice. I was not behind the wheel. No one thought about me. Which is why they all panicked when Zoë asked her grandparents if she could see me. You see, no one had accounted for my whereabouts. The Twins immediately called Mark Fein, who immediately called Denny.

"Tell her of course she can see Enzo," Denny said calmly. "Enzo is staying with Mike and Tony while I'm in Europe; Zoë likes them, and she'll believe it. I'll have Mike bring Enzo over on Saturday."

And that's what happened. In the early afternoon Mike picked me up and drove me over to Mercer Island, and I spent the afternoon playing with Zoë on the great lawn. Before dinnertime, Mike returned me to Denny.

"How did she look?" Denny asked Mike.

"She looked terrific," Mike said. "She has her mother's smile."

"They had a good time together?" asked Denny.

"A fantastic time," replied Mike. "They played all day."

"Fetch?" Denny asked, thirsty for details. "Did she use the Chuckit? Or did they play chase? Eve never liked it when they played chase."

"No, mostly fetch," Mike said kindly. "You know," Mike said, "sometimes they just flopped down on the grass and cuddled together. It was really sweet."

Denny wiped his nose quickly. "Thanks, Mike," he said. "Really. Thanks a lot."

"Anytime," Mike said.

I appreciated Mike's effort to appease Denny, even though he was avoiding the truth. Or maybe Mike didn't see what I saw. Maybe he couldn't hear what I heard. Zoë's profound sadness. Her loneliness. Her whispered plans that she and I would somehow smuggle ourselves off to Europe and find her father.

That summer without Zoë was very painful for Denny. In addition to feeling isolated from his daughter, he felt his career was derailed. Though he was offered the opportunity to drive again, he was forced to decline, as the pending criminal case demanded that he remain in the state of Washington at all times. He was a prisoner of the state.

And yet.

I won't say he created the situation, but he allowed it. Because he needed to test his mettle. He wanted to know how long he could keep his foot on the accelerator before lifting. He chose this life, and therefore he chose this battle.

And I realized, as the summer matured and I frequently visited Zoë without Denny, that I was a part of this, too. I was an important part. Because on those late Saturday afternoons in July, Denny would sit with me on the back porch and quiz me. "Did you play fetch? Did you tug? Did you chase?" He would ask, "Did you cuddle?" He would ask, "How did she look? Is she eating enough fruit? Are they buying organic?"

I tried. I tried as hard as I could to form words for him, but they wouldn't come. I tried to beam my thoughts into his head. I tried to send him the pictures I saw in my mind. I twitched my ears. I cocked my head. I nodded. I pawed. Until he smiled at me and stood.

"Thanks, Enzo," he would say on those days. "You're not too tired, are you?"

I would stand and wag. I'm never too tired.

"Let's go, then."

He would grab the Chuckit and the tennis ball and walk me down to the Blue Dog Park. There we would play fetch until the light grew thin and the mosquitoes came out of hiding, thirsty for their dinner.

thirty-eight

There was an occasion that summer when Denny found a teaching engagement in Spokane and asked if the Twins could take me for the weekend; they agreed, as they had grown accustomed to my presence in their home.

I would much rather have gone to racing school with Denny, but I understood that he depended on me to take care of Zoë. Also to act as some kind of a witness on his behalf. Though I could not relate to him the details of our visits, my presence, I think, reassured him in some way.

On a Friday afternoon, I was delivered by Mike into Zoë's waiting embrace. She immediately ushered me into her room, and we played a game of dress-up together. I knew my role as jester in Zoë's court, and I was happy to play the part.

That evening Maxwell took me outside earlier than

usual, urging me to "get busy." When I came back inside, I was led to Zoë's room, which already had my bed in it. Apparently, she had requested I sleep with her. I curled into a ball and quickly dozed off.

A bit later, I woke. The lights were dim. Zoë was awake and active, encircling my bed with piles of her stuffed animals.

"They'll keep you company," she whispered to me as she surrounded me.

Seemingly hundreds of them. All shapes and sizes. I was being surrounded by teddy bears and giraffes, sharks and dogs, cats and birds and snakes. She worked steadily and I watched, until I was buried in stuffed animals. I found it somewhat amusing and touching that Zoë cared to share me with her animals in that way. I drifted off to sleep feeling protected and safe.

I awoke later in the night and saw that the wall of animals around me was quite high. Still, I was able to shift my weight and change position to make myself more comfortable. But when I did, I was shocked by a frightening sight. One of the animals. The one on top. Staring straight at me. It was the zebra.

The replacement zebra. The one she had chosen to fill in for the demon that had dismantled itself before me so long ago. The horrifying zebra of my past. The demon had returned. And though it was dark in the room, I know I saw a glint of light in its eyes.

As you can imagine, my sleep was sparse that night. The last thing I wanted was to awaken amid animal destruction because the demon had returned. I forced myself to stay awake; yet I couldn't help but drift off. Each time I opened my eyes, I found the zebra staring at me. Like a gargoyle, it stood on a cathedral of animals above me, watching. The other animals had no life; they were toys. The zebra alone knew.

I felt sluggish all day, but I did my best to keep up, and I tried to catch up on my sleep by napping quietly. To any observer, I'm sure I gave off the impression of being quite contented. But I was anxious about nightfall, concerned that, once again, the zebra would torture me with its mocking eyes.

That afternoon, as the Twins took their alcohol on the deck, as they tended to do, and Zoë watched television in the TV room, I dozed outside in the sun. And I heard them.

"I know it's for the best," Trish said. "But still, I feel badly for him."

"It's for the best," Maxwell said.

"I know. But still . . ."

"He didn't pick Zoë up when he should have," Maxwell

said sternly. "On not just one, but several occasions. He endangered her life with his reckless driving, and he caused her to get frostbite, which can cause *permanent* nerve damage! What kind of a father is he?"

I lifted my head from the warm wood of the deck and saw Trish cluck and shake her head.

"What?" Maxwell demanded.

Trish said, "From what I hear, it was a big misunderstanding."

"What you hear!" Maxwell blurted. "He didn't!"

"I know, I know," said Trish. "It's just that this has all gotten blown out of proportion."

"Are you suggesting that he is a good father?"

"No," Trish said. "But didn't you exaggerate the situation because you were certain we wouldn't get custody of Zoë?"

"I don't care about any of that," Maxwell said, waving her off. "He wasn't good enough for Eve, and he's not good enough for Zoë. And if he's stupid enough to devote so much time to that car racing that he forgets about his own daughter, then I'm going to seize the moment. Zoë will have a better childhood with us. She will have a better moral raising, a better financial raising, a better family life, and you know it, Trish. You know it!"

"I know, I know," she said, and sipped her amber

drink with the bright red cherry drowned at the bottom of the glass. "But he's not a bad person."

He poured his drink down his gullet and slapped the glass down on the teak table.

"It's time to start dinner," he said, and he went inside.

I was stunned. I had been suspicious since the beginning. But to hear the words, the coldness in Maxwell's tone. Imagine this. Imagine having your wife die suddenly of a brain cancer. Then imagine having her parents attack you mercilessly in order to gain custody of your daughter. Imagine that they exploit allegations of neglect against you. Then they hire very expensive and clever lawyers because they have much more money than you have. Imagine that they prevent you from having any contact with your six-year-old daughter for months on end. And imagine they restrict your ability to earn money to support yourself and, of course, as you hope, your daughter. How long would you last before your will was broken?

They had no idea who they were dealing with. Denny would not kneel before them. He would never quit; he would never break.

With disgust, I followed them into the house. Trish began her preparations and Maxwell took his jar of peppers from the refrigerator; inside me, a darkness brewed. Contrivers. Manipulators. They were no longer people to me. They were now the Evil Twins. Evil, horrible people who stuffed themselves with burning hot peppers in order to fuel the fire in their stomachs. When they laughed, flames shot out of their noses. They were disgusting creatures.

My anger with the Evil Twins fed my thirst for revenge. And I was not above using the tools of my dogness to exact justice. I presented myself to Maxwell as he stuffed another pepper into his mouth and chewed it with the fake teeth he removed at night. I sat before him. I lifted a paw.

"Want a treat?" he asked me, clearly surprised by my gesture.

I barked.

"Here you go, boy."

He extracted a pepper from the bottle and held it before my nose. It was a very large one, long and artificially green and smelling of chemicals. The devil's candy.

"I don't think those are good for dogs," Trish said.

"He likes them," Maxwell countered.

My first thought was to take the hot pepper and a couple of Maxwell's fingers with it. But that would have caused real problems. I likely would have been put to sleep before Mike could return to save me, so I didn't take his fingers. I did, however, take the pepper. I knew it was bad for me, that I would suffer immediate discomfort. But I knew my discomfort would pass, and I anticipated the unpleasant rebound effect, which is what I wanted. After all, I am just a stupid dog, unworthy of human scorn, without the brains to be responsible for my own bodily functions. A dumb dog.

I observed their dinner carefully because I wanted to see for myself. The Twins served Zoë some kind of chicken covered in a creamy sauce. They didn't know that while Zoë loved chicken cutlets, she never ate them with sauce, and certainly never with cream. When she didn't eat the string beans they served, Trish asked if she would like a banana instead. Zoë said yes and Trish made some banana slices. Zoë barely picked at them because they were crudely sliced and speckled with brown spots, which she always avoided.

And these agents of evil—these supposed grand-parents!—thought Zoë would be better off with them! Bah! They didn't spend a moment thinking about her welfare; after dinner, they didn't even ask why she hadn't eaten the bananas. They allowed her to leave the table having eaten almost nothing. Denny never would have allowed that. He would have prepared for her something she liked so she would continue to grow in a healthy way.

All the while I watched, I seethed. And in my stomach,

a foul brew steeped. When it was time to take me out that night, Maxwell opened the French door to the back deck and began his idiotic chanting: "Get busy, boy. Get busy."

I didn't go outside. I looked up at him and I thought about what he was doing. How he was tearing our family apart for his own selfish purposes; I thought about how he and Trish were grossly inferior guardians for my Zoë. I crouched in my stance right there, inside the house, and I unleashed a massive, soupy, pungent pile of diarrhea on his beautiful, expensive, linen-colored Berber carpet.

"What the hell?" he shouted at me. "Bad dog!"

I turned and trotted cheerfully to Zoë's room.

"Get busy, boy," I said as I left. But, of course, he couldn't hear me.

As I settled into my pile of stuffed animals, I heard Maxwell exclaim loudly and call for Trish to clean up my mess. I looked at the zebra, still perched on his throne of lifeless animal carcasses, and I growled at it very softly but very dangerously. And the demon knew. The demon knew not to mess with me that night.

Not that night, or ever again.

thirty-nine

Oh, a breath of September!

The vacations were done. The lawyers were back at work. The courts were at full staff. The postponements were finished. The truth would be had! Denny left that morning wearing the only suit he owned, a crumpled khaki two-piece from Banana Republic, and a dark tie. He looked very good.

"Mike will come by at lunch and take you for a walk," he said to me. "I don't know how long this will go."

Mike came and walked me briefly through the neighborhood so I wouldn't be lonely. Then he left again. Later that afternoon, Denny returned. He smiled down at me.

"Do I need to reintroduce you two?" he asked. And behind him was Zoë! I leapt into the air. I bounded. I *knew* it! I *knew* Denny would vanquish the Evil Twins! I felt like doing flips. Zoë had returned!

It was an amazing afternoon. We played in the yard. We ran and laughed. We hugged and cuddled. We made dinner together and sat at our table and ate. It felt so good to be together again! After dinner, they ate ice cream in the kitchen.

"Are you going back to Europe soon?" Zoë asked out of the blue.

Denny froze in place. The story had worked so well, Zoë still believed it. He sat down across from her.

"No, I'm not going back to Europe," he said.

Her face lit up. "Yay!" she cheered. "I can have my room back!"

"Actually," Denny said, "I'm afraid not yet."

Her forehead crinkled and her lips pursed as she attempted to puzzle out his statement. I was puzzled, too.

"Why not?" she asked, finally, frustration in her voice. "I want to come home."

"I know, honey, but the lawyers and judges have to make the decision on where you'll live. It's part of what happens when someone's mommy dies."

"Just *tell* them," she demanded. "Just *tell* them that I'm coming home. I don't want to live there anymore. I want to live with you and Enzo."

"It's a little more complicated than that," said Denny.

"Someone said I did something very bad. And even though I know I didn't do it, now I have to go to court and prove to everyone that I didn't do it."

Zoë thought about it for a moment. "Was it Grandma and Grandpa?" she asked.

I was very impressed with the laserlike accuracy of her inquiry.

"Not—," Denny started. "No. No, it wasn't them. But . . . they *know* about it."

"I made them love me too much," Zoë said softly, looking into her bowl of melted ice cream. "I should have been bad. I should have made them not want to keep me."

"No, honey, no," Denny said, dismayed. "Don't say that. You should shine with all of your light all the time. I'll work this out. I promise I will."

Zoë shook her head without meeting his eyes. Sadly, she went into her bedroom to play with the animals she had left behind.

Later in the evening, the doorbell rang. Denny answered it. Mark Fein was there.

"It's time," he said.

Denny nodded and called for Zoë.

"This was a major victory for us, Dennis," Mark said. "It means a lot. You understand that, right?"

Denny nodded, but he was sad. Like Zoë.

"Every other weekend, Friday after school until Sunday after dinner, she's yours," Mark said. "And every Wednesday, you pick her up after school and deliver her before eight o'clock, right?"

"Right," Denny said.

Mark Fein looked at Denny for a long time without speaking.

"I'm very proud of you," he said, finally. "I don't know what goes on in that head of yours, but you're a real competitor."

Denny breathed in deeply. "That's what I am," he agreed.

And Mark Fein took Zoë away.

As it was, we had taken only our first step. Denny had won visitation rights. But Zoë was still in the custody of the Evil Twins. Denny was still on trial for a charge he didn't deserve. Nothing had been solved.

And yet. I had seen them together. I had seen them look at each other and giggle with relief. Which reaffirmed my faith in the balance of the universe. And while I understood that we had merely successfully navigated the first turn of a very long race, I felt that things looked good for us. Denny was not one to make mistakes. And with fresh tires and a full load of fuel, he would prove a tough foe to anyone challenging him.

forty

ow quickly.

How quickly a year passes, like a mouthful of food snatched from the jaws of eternity. How quickly.

With little drama, the months slipped by, one by one, until another fall lay before us. And still, almost nothing had changed. Back and forth, round and round, the lawyers danced and played their game. It was merely a game to them. But not to us.

Denny took Zoë on schedule, every other weekend, every Wednesday afternoon. He took her to places of cultural enrichment. Art museums. Science exhibits. The zoo and the aquarium. He taught her things. And sometimes, on secret missions, he took us to the go-karts.

Ah. The electric karts. She was just big enough to fit when he took her. And she was good. She knew the karts immediately, as if she had been born to them. She was quick.

How quickly.

With little instruction, she climbed behind the wheel. She tucked her golden hair into a helmet, buckled her harness, and was off. No fear. No hesitation. No waiting.

"You ever race against her?" the worker boy asked Denny after her very first session.

"Nope," Denny replied.

"'Cause she could kick your butt," the kid said.

"I doubt it." Denny laughed.

"So take a session," the kid said. "She wins, you pay. You win, you don't pay."

"You're on," Denny said, grabbing a helmet from the rack of helmets that people can borrow—he hadn't bothered to bring his own.

They started their race, a flying start, with Denny giving Zoë a bit of an edge, taking it easy on her. For several laps he dogged her, stayed on her back tires, let her know he was there. Then he tried to pass her. And she wouldn't let him by.

She "slammed the door" on him.

He tried again to pass. She slammed the door.

Again. Same result. It was like she knew where he was at every moment. In a kart with no mirrors. Wearing a helmet that allowed no side vision. She *felt* him. She *knew*. When he made his moves, she shut him down. Every single time.

Consider that she had a tremendous advantage, being only sixty pounds to his one hundred fifty. That's a huge weight differential in karting. Still. Consider that he was a thirty-year-old semiprofessional race car driver and she was a seven-year-old newbie. Consider the possibilities.

She won the race, God bless her little soul. She "took the checkered flag" and beat her old man. And I was so happy. I was so happy that I didn't mind it when I had to wait in the car while they went into Andy's Diner for french fries and milk shakes.

How did Denny sustain himself for the duration of this ordeal? Here's how: He had a secret. His daughter was better and quicker and smarter than he was. And while the Evil Twins may have restricted his ability to see her, when he *was* allowed to see her, he received all the energy he needed to maintain his focus.

forty-one

Spring, again. We were back at the Victrola.

I slept at my master's feet on the sidewalk of Fifteenth Avenue, which had been warmed by the sun like a cooking stone. Slept and sprawled, barely lifting my head to acknowledge the occasional petting I received from the passersby. I looked like I hadn't a care in the world. In fact, I was quite nervous, as I always was at our meetings with Mark.

"This is not a conversation I like to have," Mark Fein said, leaning back on the iron chair until it groaned with fatigue. "It's one I have too often."

"I'm ready," Denny said.

"Money," said the lawyer.

Denny nodded to himself and sighed. "I've missed some invoices."

"You owe me a ton, Dennis," Mark clarified. "I've been giving you slack, but I have to cut you off."

"Give me another thirty days of slack," Denny said.

"Can't do it, friend."

"Yes, you can," Denny said firmly. "Yes. You can."

Mark sucked on his latte. "I have investigators. Paralegals. Support staff. I have to pay these people."

"Mark," Denny said. "I'm asking you for a favor. Give me thirty days."

"You'll be paid in full?" Mark asked.

"Thirty days," said Denny.

Mark finished his coffee drink and stood. "Okay. Thirty days."

"I'll pay," Denny said. "You keep working."

forty-two

The solution had been put to Denny by Mark Fein: if Denny were to quit his claim to Zoë, the custody suit would vanish. That's what Mark Fein said. As simple as that.

At one point Mark even counseled Denny that perhaps the best thing for Zoë would be to stay with her grandparents. They were better able to provide for the comforts of her childhood, as well as pay for her college education, when that became necessary. Further, he noted that a child needs a stable home environment. This, he said, could be best provided in a single housing location and with consistent schooling, preferably in the suburbs. Or at a private school in an urban neighborhood. Mark assured Denny he would settle for nothing short of a liberal visitation schedule. He spent quite a long time trying to convince Denny of these truths.

But Denny refused to yield to these ideas. He wanted his daughter and he wanted his racing career and he refused to give up one for the other.

"It's never too late," Denny said to Mark. "Things change."

Very true. Things change quickly. And, as if to prove it, Denny sold our house.

We had no money left. They had sucked him dry. Mark had threatened to cease working for Denny's defense. There was little else Denny could do. He rented a truck from U-Haul and called on his friends, and one weekend that summer, we moved all of our belongings from our house in the Central District to a one-bedroom apartment on Capitol Hill.

I loved our house. It was small, I know. But I had grown attached to my spot in the living room on the hardwood floor, which was very warm in the winter when the sun streamed in through the window. And I loved using my dog door, which Denny had installed for me so I could venture into the backyard at will. But that was no more. That was gone. From that point forward, my days were spent in an apartment with carpeting that smelled of chemicals and insulated windows that didn't breathe properly. Plus a refrigerator that hummed too loudly and seemed to work too hard to keep the food cold. And no cable TV.

Still, I tried to make the best of it. If I squeezed myself into the corner between the arm of the sofa and the sliding glass door, I could see past the building across the street. Through a narrow gap, I could see the Space Needle with its little bronze elevators that tirelessly whisked visitors from the ground to the sky and back again.

forty-three

Denny paid his account with Mark Fein. Then Denny found a new lawyer named Mr. Lawrence. Mark had spark and fire. This one had very large ears.

This one asked for a continuance, which is what you can do in the legal world if you need time to read all the paperwork. And while I understood it was necessary, I was still concerned. While it had seemed like we were getting close to the end, suddenly the horizon shot away from us. We were waiting for the legal wheels to turn, which they did, but exceedingly slowly.

Shortly after Denny began working with our new lawyer, we received more bad news. The Evil Twins were suing Denny for child support. Dastardly, is how Mark Fein had described them. So now, in addition to taking his child from him, they demanded he pay for the food they fed her?

Mr. Lawrence defended their action as a legitimate tactic, ruthless as it might be. He posed to Denny a question: "Does the end always justify the means?" And then, he answered it: "Apparently, for them, it does."

I have an imaginary friend. I call him King Karma. I know that karma is a force in this universe, and that people like the Evil Twins will receive karmic justice for their actions. I know that this justice will come when the universe deems it appropriate, and it may not be in this lifetime but in the next, or the one after that. The current consciousness of the Evil Twins may never feel the brunt of the karma they have incurred, though their souls absolutely will. I understand this concept.

But I don't like it. And so my imaginary friend does things for me. If you are mean to someone, King Karma will swoop out of the sky and call you names. If you kick someone, King Karma will bound from an alley and kick you back. If you are cruel and vicious, King Karma will administer a fitting punishment.

At night, before I sleep, I talk to my imaginary friend and I send him to the Evil Twins, and he exacts his justice. It may not be much, but it's what I can do.

Every night, King Karma gives them very bad dreams in which they are chased mercilessly by a pack of wild dogs until they awaken with a start, and are unable to fall asleep again.

forty-four

It was an especially difficult winter for me. Perhaps it was the stairs in our apartment building. Or maybe it was my arthritis catching up to me. Or maybe I was just tired of being a dog.

I so longed to shed this body, to be free of it. And, looking back, I can tell you it was my state of mind, it was my outlook on life, that attracted me to that car and attracted that car to me. We make our own destiny.

We walked back from Volunteer Park late in the night. It was not too cold and not too warm, a gentle breeze blew, and snow fell from the sky. I was unsettled by the snow, I remember. Denny often allowed me to walk home from the park without my leash, and that night I strayed too far from him. I was watching the flakes fall and gather in a thin layer on the sidewalk and on the street, which was empty of both cars and people.

"Yo, Zo!" he called. He whistled for me, his sharp whistle.

I looked up. He was on the other side of Aloha. He must have crossed without my noticing.

"Come here, boy!"

He slapped his thigh, and I bounded toward him into the street.

Suddenly Denny spotted the car and cried out, "No! Wait!"

The tires did not scream, as tires do. The ground was covered with a thin layer of snow. The tires hushed. They shushed. And then the car hit me.

So stupid, I thought. *I am so stupid. I am the stupidest dog on the planet, and I have the nerve to dream of becoming a man? I am stupid.*

"Settle down, boy." Denny's hands were on me. Warm.

"I didn't see—" said the driver of the car.

"I know," said Denny.

"He shot out—" continued the driver.

"I totally understand. I saw the whole thing," replied Denny.

Denny lifted me. Denny held me. "I'm several blocks from home. He's too heavy to carry. Will you drive me?"

"Sure, but—"

"You tried to stop. The street is snowy," Denny said calmly.

"I'm totally freaking—I've never hit a dog before."

"What just happened isn't important," Denny said. "Let's think about what's going to happen next. Get in your car."

"Yeah," the boy said. He was just a boy. A teenager. "Where should I go?"

"Everything's fine," Denny said, sliding into the backseat with me on his lap. "Take a deep breath and let's drive."

forty-five

Ayrton Senna did not have to die.

This came to me in a flash as I lay, whimpering in pain, in the backseat of Denny's car on the way to the animal hospital that night. It came to me: on the Grand Prix circuit in the town of Imola, Senna did not have to die. He could have walked away.

Saturday, the day before the race, Senna's friend Rubens Barrichello was seriously injured in an accident. Another driver, Roland Ratzenberger, was killed during a practice session. Senna was very upset about the safety conditions of the track.

People say that he was so ambivalent about that race, the San Marino Grand Prix, that he thought seriously of retiring as a driver on Sunday morning. He almost quit. He almost walked away.

But he did not walk away. He raced, that fateful first day of May in 1994. And when his car failed to turn in at the fabled Tamburello corner, his car left the track at nearly one hundred ninety miles per hour and struck a concrete barrier; he was killed instantly by a piece of metal that penetrated his helmet.

Or he died in the helicopter on the way to the hospital.

Or he died on the track, after they had pulled him out of the wreckage.

Mysterious is Ayrton Senna, in death as well as in life.

To this day, there is still great controversy over his death. The first man to reach Senna, Sidney Watkins, said: "We lifted him from the cockpit and laid him on the ground. As we did, he sighed and, although I am totally agnostic, I felt his soul departed at that moment."

What is the real truth regarding the death of Ayrton Senna, who was only thirty-four years old? I know the truth, and I will tell you now:

He was admired, loved, cheered, honored, respected. In life as well as in death. A great man. He died that day because his body had served its purpose. His soul had done what it came to do. And I knew, as Denny sped me toward the doctor, that if I had already accomplished what I set out to accomplish here on earth, I would have been killed instantly by that car.

But I was not killed. Because I was not finished. I still had work to do.

forty-six

Separate entrances for cats and dogs. That's what I remember most. I also remember the doctor painfully manipulating my hips. Then he gave me a shot and I was very much asleep.

When I awoke, I was still groggy, but no longer in pain. I heard snippets of conversation. Terms like "chronic arthritis," and "fracture of the pelvic bone." Others like "replacement surgery," and "salvage operation," "knitting," and "pain threshold," And my favorite, "old."

Denny carried me to the lobby and laid me down on the brown carpeting, which was somehow comforting in the dim room. The assistant spoke to him and said more things that were confusing to me due to my drugged state. "X-ray." "Sedative." "Examination and diagnosis." "Injection." "Pain medications." "Nighttime emergency fee." And, of course, "Eight hundred and twelve dollars."

Denny handed the assistant a credit card. He kneeled down and stroked my head. "You'll be all right, Zo," he said. "You cracked your pelvis, but it will heal. You'll just take it easy for a while, and then you'll be good as new."

"Mr. Swift?" Denny stood and returned to the counter. "Your card has been declined."

Denny stiffened. "That's not possible."

"Do you have another card?"

"Here." Denny handed him another credit card. They both watched the blue machine that took the cards, and a few moments later, the assistant shook his head.

"You've exceeded your limit."

Denny frowned and took out another card. "Here's my ATM card. It will work."

They waited again. Same result.

"That's not right," Denny said. I could hear his breath quicken, his heart beat faster. "I just deposited my paycheck. Maybe it hasn't cleared yet."

The doctor appeared from the back.

"A problem?" he asked.

"Look, I have three hundred dollars from when I deposited my check, I took some of it out in cash. Here."

Denny fanned bills in front of the doctor.

"They must be holding the rest of the check or something, waiting for it to clear," Denny said, his voice sounding panicky. "I know I have money in that account. Or I can transfer some into it tomorrow morning from my savings."

"Relax, Denny," the doctor said. "I'm sure it's just a misunderstanding."

He said to the assistant, "Write Mr. Swift a receipt for the three hundred, and leave a note for Susan to run the card in the morning for the balance."

The assistant reached out and took Denny's cash. Denny watched closely as the young man wrote up the receipt.

"Could I keep twenty of it?" Denny asked hesitantly. I could see his lip quivering. He was exhausted and shaken and embarrassed. "I need to put some gas in my car."

The assistant looked to the doctor, who lowered his eyes and nodded silently and turned away, calling good night over his shoulder. The assistant handed Denny a twenty-dollar bill and a receipt, and Denny carried me to the car.

When we got home and Denny placed me on my bed, he sat in the dark room, lit only by the streetlamps outside, and he held his head in his hands for a long time.

"I can't keep going," he said to me. "They won. Do

you see? I can't even afford to take care of you. I can't even afford gas for my car. I've got nothing left, Enzo. There's nothing left."

Oh, how I wished I could speak. How I wished for thumbs. I could have grabbed his shirt collar. I could have pulled him close to me and I could have said to him, "This is just a crisis. A flash! You are the one who taught me to never give up. You taught me that new possibilities emerge for those who are prepared, for those who are ready. You have to believe!" But I couldn't say that. I could only look at him.

"I tried," he said. "You are my witness. I tried."

If I could have stood on my hind legs. If I could have raised my hands and held him. If I could have spoken to him. But he could not hear me. Because I am what I am. I am a dog.

And so he returned his head to his hands and he sat. I provided nothing. He was alone.

forty-seven

Days later. A week. Two. I don't know. After Denny's crisis, time meant little to me; he looked sickly, he had no energy, no life force, and so neither did I. At a point when my hips still bothered me, we went to visit Mike and Tony. We sat in their kitchen, Denny with a cup of tea and a manila folder before him. Tony wasn't present. Mike paced nervously.

"It's the right decision, Den," Mike said. "I totally support you. Mr. Lawrence got you everything you asked for: the same visitation schedule but with two weeks in the summer and one week over Christmas break, and the February school break; you don't have to pay support anymore; they'll put her in a private school on Mercer Island and they'll pay for her college education."

Denny nodded.

"And they'll withdraw the charge," Mike said.

Denny stared dully at the folder on the table.

"Denny," Mike said seriously, "you're a smart guy. One of the smartest guys I've ever met. Let me tell you, this is a smart decision. You know that, right?"

Denny looked confused for a moment, scanned the tabletop, checked his own hands.

"I need a pen," he said.

Mike reached behind him to the telephone table and picked up a pen. He handed it to Denny.

Denny hesitated, his hand poised over the documents in the folder. He looked up at Mike.

"I feel like they've sliced open my guts, Mike. Like they've sliced me open and cut out my intestines. For the rest of my life I'll have to think about how they cut me open and gutted me and I just lay there with a dead smile on my face and said, 'Well, at least I'm not broke.'"

Mike seemed at a loss. "It's rough," he said.

"Yeah," Denny agreed. "It's rough. Nice pen."

Denny held up the pen. It was one of those souvenir pens with the sliding thing in the plastic top with the liquid.

"Woodland Park Zoo," Mike said.

I looked closer. The top of the pen. A little plastic

savannah. The sliding thing? A zebra. When Denny tipped the pen, the zebra slid across the plastic savannah. The zebra is everywhere.

I suddenly realized. The zebra. It is not something outside of us. The zebra is something inside of us. Our fears. Our own self-destructive nature. The zebra is the worst part of us when we are face-to-face with our worst times. The demon is us!

Denny brought the tip of the pen to the paper and I could see the zebra sliding forward, inching toward the signature line. Then I knew it wasn't Denny who was signing. It was the zebra! Denny would never give up his daughter for a few weeks of summer vacation and to be free from child support payments!

I was an old dog. Recently hit by a car. And yet I mustered what I could, and the pain medication Denny had given me earlier helped with the rest. I pushed up onto his lap with my paws. I reached out with my teeth. And the next thing I knew, I was standing at the kitchen door with the papers in my mouth and both Mike and Denny staring at me, completely stunned.

"Enzo!" Denny commanded. "Drop it!"

I refused.

"Enzo! Drop!" he yelled.

"Come here, boy!" Mike said.

I looked over at him; he was holding a banana. Which was totally unfair. He knew how much I loved bananas. But still, I refused.

"Enzo, get the heck over here!" Denny shouted, and he lunged at me.

I slipped away.

It was a low-speed chase, to be sure, my mobility being restricted as it was. But it was a chase nonetheless. One in which I dodged and slid and evaded the hands that grasped for my collar. I held them off.

I still had the papers, even when they cornered me in the living room. Even when they were about to catch me and wrest the papers from my jaws, I had a chance. I was trapped, I know. But Denny taught me that the race isn't over until the checkered flag flies. I looked around and noticed that one of the windows was open. It wasn't open much, and there was a screen on it, but it was open, and that was enough.

Despite all of my pain, I lunged. With all of my might, I dove. I cleared the opening; I crashed into that screen and through it. And suddenly I was on the porch. I scurried into the backyard. Mike and Denny flew out the back door, panting, and yet not pursuing. Instead, they seemed somewhat impressed by my feat.

"He dove," Mike said, breathless.

"Out the window," Denny finished for him.

Yes, I did. I dove.

"If we had a videotape of that, we could win ten thousand dollars on *America's Funniest Home Videos*," Mike said.

"Give me the papers, Enzo," Denny said.

I shook them vigorously in my mouth. Mike laughed at my refusal.

"It's not funny," Denny admonished.

"It's kind of funny," Mike replied in his defense.

"Give me the papers," Denny repeated.

I dropped the papers before me and pawed at them. I dug at them. I tried to bury them.

Again, Mike laughed.

Denny, however, was very angry; he glared at me.

"Enzo," he said, "I'm warning you."

What could I do? Had I not made myself clear? Had I not communicated my message? What else was there for me to do?

One thing only. I lifted my hind leg and I peed on the papers. Gestures are all that I have.

When they saw what I had done, they couldn't help

themselves; they laughed. Denny and Mike. They laughed so hard. Denny laughed harder than I'd seen him laugh in years. Their faces turned red. They could barely breathe. They fell to their knees and laughed until they could laugh no more.

"Okay, Enzo," Denny said. "It's okay."

I went to him then, leaving the soaked papers on the grass.

"Call Lawrence," Mike said to Denny. "He'll print them again and you can sign them."

Denny stood.

"No," he said, "I'm with Enzo. I piss on their settlement, too. I don't care how smart it is for me to sign it. I didn't do anything wrong, and I'm not giving up. I'm never giving up."

"They're going to be mad," Mike said with a sigh.

"Screw them," Denny said. "I'm going to win this thing or I'm going to run out of fuel on the last lap. But I'm not going to quit. I promised Zoë. I'm not going to quit."

When we got home, Denny gave me a bath and toweled me off. Afterward, he turned on the TV in the living room.

"What's your favorite?" he asked, looking at the shelf

of videotapes he kept, all the races we loved to watch together. "Ah, here's one you like."

He started the tape. Ayrton Senna driving the Grand Prix of Monaco in 1984, slicing through the rain. Senna would have won that race, had they not stopped it because of the conditions; when it rained, it never rained on Senna.

We watched the race together without pause, side by side, Denny and me.

forty-eight

The summer of my tenth birthday came along and there was a sense of balance to our lives, though none of completeness. We still spent alternate weekends with Zoë. She had grown so tall recently, and never let a moment pass without questioning an assumption, challenging a theory, or offering an insight that made Denny smile with pride.

My hips had healed poorly from my accident, but I was determined not to cost Denny any more money. I pushed through the pain, which at times prevented me from sleeping through the nights. I tried my best to keep up with the pace of life; my mobility was severely limited and I couldn't gallop or canter, but I could still trot fairly well.

Money was still a constant struggle for us, since

Denny had to give the Evil Twins a portion of his pay-check. Fortunately, Denny's bosses were generous in allowing him to change his schedule frequently so he could teach driving on certain days at Pacific Raceways. This was an easy way for Denny to make more money to pay for his defense.

Sometimes, on his driving school days, Denny would take me with him to the track. While I was never allowed to ride with him, I did enjoy sitting in the stands and watching him teach. I became known as a bit of a track dog, and I especially liked trotting through the paddock, looking at the latest fashions in cars. From the nimble Lotus to the classic Porsche to the more flamboyant Lamborghini, there was always something good to see.

On a hot day at the end of July, while they were all out on the course, I watched as a beautiful red Ferrari F430 drove through the paddock and up to the school headquarters. A small, older man climbed out, and the owner of the school, Don Kitch, came to meet him. They embraced and spoke for several minutes.

The man strolled to the bleachers to get a view of the track, and Don radioed to his corner workers to end the session and bring in the students for lunch break. As the drivers climbed out of their vehicles, Don called for

Denny, who approached, as did I, curious about what was going on.

"I need a favor," Don said to Denny.

And suddenly the small man with the Ferrari was with us.

"You remember Luca Pantoni, don't you?" Don asked. "We came to dinner at your place a couple of years ago."

"Of course," Denny said, shaking Luca's hand.

"Your wife cooked a delightful dinner," Luca said. "I remember it still. Please accept my sincere and heartfelt condolences."

When I heard him speak with his Italian accent, I recognized him immediately. The man from Ferrari.

"Thank you," Denny said quietly.

"Luca would like you to show him our track," Don said.

"No problem," Denny said, pulling on his helmet and walking to the passenger side of the exquisite automobile.

"Mr. Swift," Luca called out. "Perhaps you would do me the favor of allowing me to be the passenger so that I may see more."

Surprised, Denny looked at Don. "You want me to drive *this* car?" he asked. After all, the F430 is priced at nearly a quarter of a million dollars.

"I accept full liability," Luca said.

"I'd be pleased to," Denny said, and he climbed into the cockpit.

It was an extremely beautiful car, and it was outfitted not for street use, but for the track. It had ceramic brake rotors, one-piece racing seats, and harnesses and F1-style paddle shifters. The two men strapped in, and Denny pressed the electronic start button, and the car fired to life.

Ah, what a sound. The whine of the fantastic engine layered over the throaty rumble of the massive exhaust. Denny flicked the paddle shifter, and they cruised slowly through the paddock toward the track entrance.

I followed Don into the school classroom, where the students were eating lunch.

"If you drivers want to see something special," Don said, "grab your sandwiches and come out to the bleachers. There's a lunch session going on."

The Ferrari was the only car on the track, as the track was usually closed during the lunch hour. But this was a special occasion.

"What's going on?" one of the other instructors asked Don.

"Denny's got an audition," Don replied mysteriously. We all went out to the bleachers in time to see Denny come around turn 9 and streak down the straight.

"I figure it will take him three laps to learn the sequential shifter," Don said.

Sure enough, Denny started slowly, like he had driven with me back at Thunderhill. Oh, how I wished I could have traded places with Luca, that lucky dog! To be copilot to Denny in an F430 must be an amazing experience.

He was driving easy, but as he came around for the third time, there was a noticeable change to the car. It was no longer a car, it was a red blur. It no longer whined, it screamed as it shot down the straightaway. It was so fast that the students laughed at each other as if someone had just told a dirty joke. Denny was laying down a hot lap.

A minute later, the Ferrari popped out of the cluster of trees at turn 7, cresting the rise until its suspension was totally extended. Then with a *pock-pock-pock* sound we heard the electronic clutch quickly downshift from sixth to third. We saw the ceramic brake rotors glow red between the spokes of the magnesium wheels. Then we heard the throttle open full and watched the car slam through the sweeping turn 8 as if it were a rocket sled, as if it were on rails. The Ferrari's hot rubber racing tires grabbed the greasy pavement like Velcro, and then—*pock!*—the car was shifting up and—*pock!*—blasting past us no more than two inches from the concrete barrier. The Doppler effect of the passing car converted its snarl into an angry growl, and off it rocketed—*pock!*—shifting again and it was gone.

"Holy cow!" a student said.

I looked back at them, and their mouths were agape. We all were silent, and we could hear that sound—*pock, pock*—as Denny set himself up for turn 5A on the back side of the track, which we couldn't see but which we could imagine, and again Denny careened past us at a million miles an hour.

"How close to the edge is he?" someone asked aloud.

Don smiled and shook his head. "He's way past the edge," he said. "I'm sure Luca told him to show him what he could do, and that's what he's doing." Then he turned to the group and shouted, "Don't you ever drive like that! Denny is a professional race car driver and that's not his car! He doesn't have to pay for it if he breaks it!"

Lap after lap, around they went until we were dizzy and exhausted from watching them. And then the car slowed considerably—a cool-down lap—and pulled off into the paddock.

The entire class gathered around as Denny and Luca emerged from the burning hot vehicle. The students were abuzz; they touched the scalding glass window that shielded the magnificent engine and exclaimed at the spectacular drive.

"Everyone into the classroom!" Don barked. "We'll go over corner notes from your morning sessions."

As they headed off, Don clasped Denny's shoulder firmly.

"What was it like?"

"It was incredible," Denny said.

"Good for you. You deserve it."

Don went off to teach his class; Luca approached and extended his hand. In it was a business card.

"I would like you to work for me," Luca said with his thick accent.

I sat next to Denny, who reached down and scratched my ear out of habit.

"I appreciate that," Denny said. "But I don't think I'd make a very good car salesman."

"Neither do I," Luca said.

"But you're with Ferrari," replied Denny.

"Yes. I work in Maranello, at Ferrari headquarters. We have a wonderful track there."

"I see," Denny said. "So you'd like me to work . . . where?"

"At the track," replied Luca. "There is some need, as often our clients would like track instruction in their new cars."

"Instructing?"asked Denny.

"There is some need," Luca replied. "But mostly, you would be testing the vehicles."

Denny's eyes got extremely large and he sucked in a huge breath of air, as did I. Was this guy saying what we thought he was saying?

"In Italy," Denny said.

"Yes," said Luca. "You would be provided with an apartment for you and your daughter. And of course, a company car—a Fiat—as part of your compensation package."

"To live in Italy," Denny said. "And test-drive Ferraris."

"*Sí.*"

Denny rolled his head around. He turned around in a circle, looked down at me, laughed.

"Why me?" Denny asked. "There are a thousand guys who can drive this car."

"Don Kitch tells me you are an exceptional driver in the wet weather," Luca replied.

"I am. But that can't be the reason."

"No," Luca said. "You are correct." He stared at Denny, his clear blue eyes smiling. "But I would prefer to tell you more about those reasons when you join me in Maranello, and I can invite you to my house for dinner."

Denny nodded and chewed his lip. He tapped Luca's business card against his thumbnail. "I appreciate your generous offer," he said. "But I'm afraid certain things prevent me from leaving this country—or even this state—at the moment. So I have to decline."

"I know about your troubles," Luca said. "That is why I am here."

Denny looked up, surprised.

"I will keep the position available for you until your situation is resolved and you can make your decision free from the burden of circumstance. My telephone number is on my card."

Luca smiled and shook Denny's hand again. He slipped into the Ferrari.

"I wish you would tell me why," Denny said.

Luca held up his finger. "Dinner, at my home. You will understand."

He drove away.

Denny shook his head in bewilderment as the high-performance driving school students emerged from the classroom and headed for their cars. Don appeared.

"Well?" he asked.

"I don't understand," Denny said.

"He's taken an interest in your career since he first met you," Don said. "Whenever we talk, he asks how you're doing."

"Why does he care so much?" Denny asked.

"He wants to tell you himself," replied Don. "All I can say is that he respects how you're fighting for your daughter."

Denny thought for a moment. "But what if I don't win?" he asked.

"There is no dishonor in losing the race," Don said. "There is only dishonor in not racing because you are afraid to lose." He paused. "Now get the heck out on the track! That's where you belong!"

forty-nine

"You need to go out? Let's go out."

He was holding my leash. He wore his jeans and a light jacket for the fall chill. He lifted me to my unsteady feet and clipped on the leash. We went out into the darkness; I had fallen asleep early, but it was time for me to pee.

I had been experiencing a decline in my health. Once I was up and moving, once I had warmed up my joints and ligaments, I felt fine and was able to move well. However, whenever I slept or lay in one spot for any amount of time, my hind joints locked in place. Then I found it difficult to get them moving again, or even to rise to a standing position.

That evening—it was around ten, I knew, because *The Amazing Race* had just finished—Denny took me out. The night was bracing, and I enjoyed the feeling of wakefulness as I breathed in through my nostrils. The energy.

We crossed Pine Street and I saw people smoking outside the Cha Cha Lounge. I forced myself to ignore the urge to sniff the gutter. And yet I peed on the street like an animal because that was the only alternative I was given. To be a dog.

We walked down Pine toward the city, and then she was there.

Both of us stopped. We held our breaths. Two older women at an outdoor table at Bauhaus Books and Coffee, and one of them was Trish, the female Evil Twin.

Liar! Schemer! Witch!

How awful for us to have to see this horrid person. I wanted to leap at her and take her nose in my teeth and twist! How I hated this woman who had brought such misery to my Denny. How I despised she who would rend this family because of her own agenda. How my anger burned.

At Bauhaus, she sat at an outdoor table with another woman. I thought we would cross the street to avoid a confrontation, but instead, we headed straight for her. I didn't understand. Perhaps Denny hadn't seen her. Perhaps he didn't know?

But I knew, and so I resisted. I set my weight, I ducked my head.

"Come on, boy," Denny ordered me. He tugged at my leash. I refused. "With me!" he snapped.

No! I would not go with him!

And then he leaned down. He kneeled and held my muzzle and looked me in the eyes.

"I see her, too," he said. "Let's handle this with dignity." He released my muzzle.

"This can work *for* us, Zo. I want you to go up to her and love her more than you've ever loved anyone before."

I didn't understand his strategy, but I gave in. After all, he had the leash.

As we drew abreast of her table, Denny stopped and looked surprised.

"Oh, hey!" he said brightly.

Trish looked up, feigning shock, clearly having seen us, but hoping there would be no interaction.

"Denny."

I played my part. I greeted her enthusiastically, I nuzzled her, I pushed my nose into her leg, I sat and looked at her with great anticipation, which is something people find very appealing. But inside, I was churning. *Yuck.*

"Good to see you, Enzo!" she said.

"Hey," Denny said, "can we talk for a minute?"

Trish's friend stood up. "I'll go get more coffee," she said as she went into the café.

"Trish," Denny said.

"Denny."

He pulled up a chair from the next table, which was empty. He sat down next to her.

"I completely understand your point of view," he said.

Trish looked surprised.

"I understand that you love Zoë and want to make sure she grows up to be as wonderful a woman as Eve was. I understand that."

"Thank you for understanding," Trish said.

"I know that I'm far from perfect. I admit I've messed up a few times, and I can see how that would make you skeptical of me as a parent."

"Yes, well—"

"But, Trish, you have to believe this: I love Zoë more than anything else in this entire world. I love her as much as you and Maxwell loved Eve. I really do. And I would *never* do anything to hurt her, put her in danger, or make her suffer for even an instant. You could never find a better champion of your granddaughter than me if you spent all of eternity looking. Please, Trish, don't take her away from me."

Trish didn't look up from her coffee, but I glanced at her. Tears hung on her lower lids.

We paused a moment, and then we turned and walked

away briskly, and Denny's gait seemed lighter than it had been for years.

"I think she heard me," he said. I thought so, too, but how could I respond? I barked twice.

He looked at me and laughed. "Faster?" he asked.

I barked twice again.

"Faster, then," he said. "Let's go!" And we trotted the rest of the way home.

fifty

The couple who stood in the doorway were entirely foreign to me. They were old and frail. They wore threadbare clothing. They toted old fabric suitcases that bulged awkwardly. They smelled of mothballs and coffee. Denny's parents had come to visit at last.

Denny embraced the woman and kissed her cheek. He picked up her bag with one hand and shook the man's hand with the other. They shuffled into the apartment and Denny took their coats.

"Your room is in here," he said to them, carrying their bags into the bedroom. "I'll sleep on the sofa."

Neither of them said a word. He was bald except for a crescent of stringy black hair. His skull was long and narrow. His eyes were sunken like his cheeks; his face was covered with a gray bristle that looked painful. The woman had white hair that was quite thin and left most of her scalp visible. She wore sunglasses, even in the apartment, and she often stood completely still and waited until the man was next to her before she moved.

She whispered into the man's ear.

"Your mother would like to use the washroom," the man said.

"*I'll* show her," Denny said. He stood next to the woman and held out his arm.

"I'll show her," the man said. The woman took the man's arm, and he led her toward the hall where the bathroom was.

"The light switch is hidden behind the hand towel," Denny said.

"She doesn't need a light switch," the man said.

That's when I realized Denny's mother was blind.

As they went into the bathroom, Denny turned away and rubbed his face with the palms of his hands.

"Good to see you," he said into his hands. "It's been so long."

fifty-one

Had I known I was meeting Denny's parents, I might
have acted more receptive to these strangers. I
had been given no advance notice, no warning, and so
my surprise was completely justified. Still, I would have
preferred to greet them like family.

They stayed with us for three days, and they hardly
left the apartment. For the afternoon on one of those
days, Denny retrieved Zoë, who was so pretty with her
hair in ribbons and a nice dress. She had obviously been
coached by Denny. She willingly sat for quite a long time
on the couch and allowed Denny's mother to explore her
face with her hands. Tears ran down Denny's mother's
cheeks during the entire encounter, raindrops spotting
Zoë's flower-print dress.

Our meals were prepared by Denny, and were simple

in nature: broiled steaks, steamed string beans, boiled potatoes. They were eaten in silence. The fact that three people could occupy such a small apartment and speak so few words was quite strange to me.

Denny's father lost some of his gruff edge while he was with us, and he even smiled at Denny a few times. Once, in the silence of the apartment, while I sat in my corner watching the Space Needle elevators, he came and stood behind me.

"What do you see, boy?" he asked quietly, and he touched the crown of my head and his fingers scratched at my ears just the way Denny does. How the touch of a son is so like the touch of his father.

I looked back at him.

"You take good care of him," he said.

And I couldn't tell if he was talking to me or to Denny. And if he was talking to me, did he mean it as a command or as an acknowledgment? The human language, as precise as it is with its thousands of words, can still be so wonderfully vague.

On the last night of their visit, Denny's father handed Denny an envelope. "Open it," he said.

Denny did as instructed, and looked at the contents.

"Where the heck did this come from?" he asked.

"It came from us," his father replied.

"You don't have any money."

"We have a house. We have a farm."

"You can't sell your house!" Denny exclaimed.

"We didn't," his father said. "It's a kind of bank loan. The bank will get our house when we die, but we thought you needed the money now more than you would later, so."

Denny looked up at his father, who was quite tall and very thin; his clothes draped on him like clothes on a scarecrow.

"Dad—" Denny started, but his eyes filled with tears and he could only shake his head. His father reached for him and embraced him. He held him close and stroked his hair with long fingers and fingernails that had large, pale half-moons.

"We never did right by you," his father said. "We never did right. This makes it right."

They left the next morning. Like the last strong autumn wind that rattles the trees until the remaining leaves fall, brief but powerful was their visit, signaling that the season had changed, and soon, life would begin again.

fifty-two

So much information came out in the following days, thanks to Mike. He plagued Denny with questions until he answered. About his mother's blindness, which came on when Denny was a boy; he cared for her until he left home after high school. About how his father told Denny that if he didn't stay to help with the farm and his mother, he shouldn't bother keeping in touch at all. About how Denny called every Christmas for years until his mother finally answered the phone and listened without speaking. For years, until she finally asked how he was doing and if he was happy.

I learned that his parents had not paid for the testing program in France, as Denny had claimed; he paid for that with a home equity loan. I learned that his parents had not contributed to the sponsorship of the touring car season, as Denny had said; he paid for that with a second mortgage, which Eve had encouraged.

Always pushing the extremes. Finding himself broke. And finding himself on the telephone with his blind mother, asking her for some kind of help so that he could keep his daughter; her response that she would give him everything if only she could meet her grandchild. Her hands on Zoë's hopeful face; her tears on Zoë's dress.

"Such a sad story," Mike said, pouring himself another soda.

"Actually," Denny said, examining his can of Diet Coke, "I believe it has a happy ending."

fifty-three

"All rise," the bailiff called out, such old-fashioned formality in such a contemporary setting. The new Seattle courthouse, with its glass walls and metal beams jutting out at all angles, was lit by a strange, bluish light.

"The Honorable Judge Van Tighem."

An elderly man, clad in a black robe, strode into the room. He was short and wide, and he had a wave of gray hair swept to one side of his head. His dark, bushy eyebrows hung over his small eyes like hairy caterpillars; he spoke with an Irish lilt.

"Sit," he commanded. "Let us begin."

Thus, the trial commenced. At least in my mind. I won't give you all the details because I don't know them. I wasn't there because I am a dog, and dogs are not allowed in court. The only impressions I have of the trial are the fantastic images and scenes I invented in my dreams. The only facts I know are the ones I gathered from Denny's retelling of events; my only idea of a courtroom, as I have said before, is what I learned from watching my favorite movies and television shows. I pieced together those days as one puts together a partially completed jigsaw puzzle. The frame is finished, the corners filled in, but handfuls of the heart and belly are missing.

The first two days were devoted to trial preparations. Denny and Mike didn't talk much about those events, so I assume everything went as expected. Both days, Tony and Mike arrived at our apartment early in the morning; Mike escorted Denny to court while Tony stayed behind to look after me.

On the third morning, there was a definite change in the air when Tony and Mike arrived. There was much more tension, fewer pleasantries, no joking around. It was the day the case was to begin in earnest, and we were all nervous. Denny's future was at stake, and it was no laughing matter.

Apparently, I later learned, Denny's lawyer, Mr. Lawrence, delivered an impassioned opening statement. He agreed with the prosecution's assertion that criminal neglect is a serious crime, but he pointed out that baseless allegation is an equally destructive weapon. And he pledged to prove Denny innocent of the charges against him.

The prosecution led off their case with a parade of witnesses. One by one, they depicted a world in which Denny showed a callous disregard for Zoë's care and well-being. How he abandoned the family at important times to pursue his passion for racing cars. How Denny hadn't even been present at the birth of his daughter. Each convincing witness was followed by another even more convincing, and another after that. Until, finally, the grandmother, Trish, was called to take the stand.

Early that afternoon—it was Wednesday—the weather was oppressive. The clouds were heavy, but the sky refused to rain. Tony and I walked down to Bauhaus so he could get his coffee. We sat outside and stared at the traffic on Pine Street until my mind shut down and I lost track of time.

"Enzo—"

I raised my head. Tony pocketed his cell phone.

"That was Mike. The prosecutor asked for a special recess. Something's going on."

He paused, waiting for my response. I said nothing.

"What should we do?" he asked.

I barked twice. We should go.

Tony closed up his computer and got his bag together. We hurried down Pine and across the freeway overpass. He was moving very quickly, and I had a hard time keeping up. When he felt the leash go taut, he looked back at me and slowed. "We have to hurry if we want to catch them," he said. I wanted to catch them, too. But my hips ached so. We hustled past the Paramount Theater to Fifth Avenue. We rushed south, zigzagging from WALK to DON'T WALK signals until we reached the plaza before the courthouse on Third Avenue.

Mike and Denny were not there. Only a small cluster of people in one corner of the plaza, speaking urgently, gesturing with agitation. We started toward them. Perhaps they knew what was going on. But at that moment, the rain began to fall. The group immediately disbanded, and I saw Trish among them. Her face was drawn and pale. When she saw me, she winced, turned away quickly, and vanished into the building.

Why was she so upset? I didn't know, but it made me very nervous. What could be going on inside that building, in the dark chambers of justice? What might she have said to further incriminate Denny and destroy his life? How I prayed for some kind of intervention, for the spirit of Truth to step out of a passing bus and deliver a rousing speech that would set everything right.

Tony and I took refuge underneath an awning; we stood tensely. Something was going on, and I didn't know what it was. I wished that I could have injected myself into the process, snuck into the courtroom, leapt on a table, and made my voice heard. But my participation was not part of the plan.

"It's done now," Tony said. "We can't change what's already been decided."

My legs were so heavy I could no longer stand; I lay on the wet concrete, and I fell into an unsteady sleep filled with very strange dreams.

"It's over."

My master's voice. I opened my eyes. Denny was flanked by Mike and Mr. Lawrence, who held a very large umbrella. How much time had passed, I didn't know. But Tony and I were both very wet from the rain.

"That recess was the longest forty-five minutes of my life," Denny said.

I waited for his answer.

"She changed her whole story," he said. "They dropped the custody suit."

He fought it, I know, but it was hard for him to breathe.

"They dropped the suit and I get Zoë."

Denny might have been able to hold off the tears if we had been alone, but Mike wrapped him in a hug. And that's when Denny unleashed the years of tears that had been dammed up. He cried so hard.

"Thank you, Mr. Lawrence," Tony said, shaking Mr. Lawrence's hand. "You did a fantastic job."

Mr. Lawrence smiled, perhaps for the first time in his life.

"All they had was the grandparents' testimony," he said. "And some of it seemed so overblown. I could tell Trish was wavering. There was something more she wanted to say. So I went after her and she broke down. She said that up until now she'd been telling people what her husband told her to say."

The lawyer continued, "She said that Denny wasn't a bad father. They had used an unfortunate event and blown it way out of proportion. Once they started, it snowballed and it was hard to stop. She said she just wanted things to go back to the way they were, with Denny having full custody of Zoë. She only asked that they be able to see their granddaughter as they did before. After that, there was nothing left to say."

So Trish saved Denny. I wondered where she was, what she was thinking. I glanced around the plaza and spotted her leaving the courthouse with Maxwell. She seemed somehow fragile.

She looked over and saw us. She was not a bad person, I knew then. One can never be angry at another driver for a track incident. One can only be upset at himself for being caught in the wrong place at the wrong time.

She gave a quick wave meant for Denny, but I was the only one who saw because I was the only one looking. So I barked to let her know.

"You've got a good master, there," Tony said to me, his attention still on our immediate circle.

He was right. I have the best master.

I watched Denny as he held on to Mike and swayed back and forth, feeling the relief, the release. Knowing that another path might have been easier for him to travel, but that it couldn't possibly have offered a more satisfying conclusion.

fifty-four

The very next day, Mr. Lawrence informed Denny that the Evil Twins had requested forty-eight hours to assemble Zoë and her belongings and spend a little more time with her before delivering her to Denny; he was under no obligation to agree.

Denny could have been mean. He could have been spiteful. They took years of his life, they took all of his money. They robbed him of work and they tried to destroy him. But Denny is a gentleman. Denny has compassion for his fellow man. He granted them their request.

He was baking cookies last night in anticipation of Zoë's return, making the batter from scratch like he used to do, when the phone rang. Since his hands were covered with sticky oatmeal goop, he tapped the speaker button on the kitchen phone.

"You're on the air!" he said brightly. "Thanks for calling. What's on your mind?" There was a long pause filled with static.

"I'm calling for Dennis Swift."

"This is Denny," Denny called from his cookie bowl. "How can I help you?"

"This is Luca Pantoni, returning your call. From Maranello. Am I catching you at a bad time?"

Denny's eyebrows shot up, he smiled at me.

"Luca! *Grazie*, for returning my call. I'm making cookies, so I have you on the speakerphone. I hope you don't mind."

"No problem."

"Luca, the reason I called . . . The issues that were keeping me in the States have been resolved."

"I can tell by the tone of your voice they were resolved to your satisfaction," Luca observed.

"Very much so," Denny said. "Yes, indeed. I was wondering if the position you offered me earlier was still available?"

"Of course."

"My daughter and I—and my dog, Enzo—would very much like to join you for dinner in Maranello, then."

"Your dog is named Enzo? How appropriate!"

"He is a race car driver at heart," Denny said, and he

smiled at me. I love Denny so much. I know everything about him, and yet he always surprises me. He called Luca!

"I look forward to meeting your daughter and to seeing Enzo again," Luca said. "I will have my assistant make the arrangements. It will be necessary to retain your services under contract. I hope you understand. The nature of our business, as well as the expense of developing a test driver—"

"I understand," Denny replied, plopping oatmeal and raisins onto the cookie sheet.

"You do not object to a three-year commitment?" Luca asked. "Your daughter will not mind living here? There is an American school, if she would prefer it to our Italian schools."

"She told me she wants to try the Italian school," Denny said. "We'll have to see how it goes. Either way, she knows it will be a great adventure, and she's very excited. She's been studying a children's book I gave her that teaches some simple Italian phrases. She says she feels confident ordering pizza in Maranello, and she loves pizza."

"*Bene!* I love pizza, too! I like the way your daughter thinks, Denny. I am so pleased I can be a part of your fresh start."

Denny plopped more cookies, almost as if he had forgotten about the telephone call.

"My assistant will be in touch with you, Denny. We will expect to see you in a few weeks."

"Yes, Luca, thank you." *Plop, plop.* "Luca."

"*Sí?*"

"Now will you tell me why you offered me the job?" Denny asked.

Luca said, "I will tell you. Many years ago, when my wife passed away, I almost died from grief."

"I'm sorry," Denny said, no longer working the cookie batter, simply listening.

"Thank you," Luca said. "It took me a long time to know how to respond to people offering their condolences. Such a simple thing, yet filled with much pain. I'm sure you understand."

"I do," Denny said.

"I *would* have died from grief, Denny, if I had not received help. If I had not found someone who offered me his hand. Do you understand? My boss at this company offered me a job driving cars for him. He saved my life. Not merely for me, but for my children as well. This man passed away recently—he was very old. But still, sometimes I see his face, I hear his voice, and I remember him. What he offered me is not for me to keep, but for me to give to another. That is why I feel very fortunate that I am able to offer my hand to you."

Denny stared at the phone as if he could see Luca in it.

"Thank you, Luca, for your hand, and for telling me why you have offered it."

"My friend," Luca said, "the pleasure is entirely mine. Welcome to Ferrari. I assure you, you will not want to leave."

They said their good-byes, and Denny pressed the button with his pinkie. He crouched down and held out his sticky hands for me, and I obligingly licked them clean.

"Sometimes I believe," he said to me as I indulged in the sweetness of his hands, of his fingers, of his opposable thumbs. "Sometimes I really do believe."

fifty-five

The dawn breaks gently on the horizon and spills its light over the land. My life seems like it has been so long and so short at the same time. People speak of a will to live. They rarely speak of a will to die. Because people are afraid of death. Death is dark and unknown and frightening. But not for me. It is not the end.

I can hear Denny in the kitchen. I can smell what he's doing; he's cooking breakfast, something he used to do all the time when we were a family, when Eve was with us and Zoë. For a long time they have been gone, and Denny has eaten cereal.

With every bit of strength I have in my body, I wrench myself to a standing position. Though my hips are frozen and my legs burn with pain, I hobble to the door of the bedroom.

"Yo, Zo!" he calls to me when he sees me. "How are you feeling?"

"Like crap," I reply. But, of course, he doesn't hear me.

"I made you pancakes," he says, cheerfully.

I force myself to wag my tail, and I really shouldn't, because the wagging jostles my bladder and I feel warm droplets of urine splash my feet.

"It's okay, boy," he says. "I've got it."

He cleans up my mess and tears me a piece of pancake. I take it in my mouth, but I can't chew it, I can't taste it. It sits on my tongue limply until it finally falls out of my mouth and onto the floor. I think Denny notices, but he doesn't say anything; he keeps flipping the pancakes, setting them on the rack to cool.

I don't want Denny to worry about me. I don't want to force him to take me on a one-way visit to the vet. He loves me so much. The worst thing I could possibly do to Denny is make him hurt me.

When I return to this world, I will be a man. I will walk among you. I will lick my lips with my small tongue. I will shake hands with other men, grasping firmly with my opposable thumbs. And I will teach people all that I know. And when I see a man or a woman or a child in trouble, I will offer my hand. To him. To her. To you. To the world. I will be a good citizen, a good partner in the endeavor of life that we all share.

I go to Denny, and I push my muzzle into his thigh.

"There's my Enzo," he says.

And he reaches down out of instinct; we've been together so long, he touches the crown of my head, and his fingers scratch at the crease of my ears. The touch of a man.

My legs buckle and I fall.

"Zo?" He is alarmed. He crouches over me. "Are you okay?"

I am fine. I am wonderful. I am. I am.

"Zo?"

He turns off the fire under the frying pan. He places his hand over my heart. The beating that he feels, if he feels anything at all, is not strong.

In the past few days, everything has changed. He is going to be reunited with Zoë. I would like to see that moment. They are going to Italy together. To Maranello. They will live in an apartment in the small town, and they will drive a Fiat. Denny will be a wonderful driver for Ferrari. I can see him, already an expert on the track because he is so quick, so smart. They will see his talent and they will pluck him from the ranks of test drivers and give him a tryout for the Formula One team.

"Try me," he will say, and they will try him.

They will see his talent and make him a driver, and soon, he will be a Formula One champion just like Ayrton Senna. My Denny!

I would like to see that. All of it, beginning this afternoon when Zoë arrives and is once again together with her father. But I don't believe I will get the chance to see that moment. And, anyway, it is not for me to decide. My soul has learned what it came to learn, and all the other things are just things. We can't have everything we want. Sometimes, we simply have to believe.

"You're okay," he says. He cradles my head in his lap. I see him.

I know this much about racing in the rain. I know it is about balance. It is about anticipation and patience. I know all of the driving skills that are necessary for one to be successful in the rain. But racing in the rain is also about the *mind*! It is about believing that one's car is merely an extension of one's body. It is about believing that you are not you; you are everything. And everything is you.

Racers are often called selfish and egotistical. I myself have called race car drivers selfish; I was wrong. To be a champion, you must have no ego at all. You must not exist as a separate entity. You must give yourself over to the race. You are nothing if not for your team, your car, your shoes, your tires. Do not mistake confidence and self-awareness for egotism.

I saw a documentary once. It was about dogs in Mongolia.

It said that the next incarnation for a dog—a dog who is ready to leave his dogness behind—is as a man.

I am ready.

And yet . . .

Denny is so very sad; he will miss me so much. I would rather stay with him and Zoë here in the apartment and watch the people on the street below as they talk to each other and shake each other's hands.

"You've always been with me," Denny says to me. "You've always been my Enzo."

Yes. I have. He's correct.

"It's okay," he says to me. "If you need to go now, you can go."

I turn my head, and there, before me, is my life. My childhood. My world.

My world is all around me. All around the fields of Spangle, where I was born. The rolling hills covered with the golden grasses that sway in the wind. They tickle my stomach when I move over them. The sky so perfectly blue and the sun so round.

This is what I would like. To play in those fields for a little longer. To spend a little more time being me before I become someone else. This is what I would like.

And I wonder: Have I squandered my dogness? Have I forsaken my nature for my desires? Have I made a mistake by anticipating my future and shunning my present?

Perhaps I have. An embarrassing deathbed regret. Silly stuff.

"The first time I saw you," he says, "I knew we belonged together."

Yes! Me, too!

"It's okay."

I feel his warm breath on my neck, his hands. He leans down to me, though I can no longer see him, he leans down to my ear.

The fields are so large I could run forever in one direction and then run forever back. There is no end to these fields.

"It's okay, boy," he says softly, gently, into my ear.

That documentary said that after a dog dies, his soul is released into the world around us. His soul is released to run in the world, run through the fields, enjoy the earth, the wind, the rivers, the rain, the sun, the—

When a dog dies, his soul is released to run until he is ready to be reborn. I remember.

"It's okay."

When I am reborn as a man, I will find Denny. I will find Zoë. I will walk up to them and shake their hands and tell them that Enzo says hello. They will see.

"You can go."

Before me I see my world: the fields around Spangle.

There are no fences. No buildings. No people. There is only me and the grass and the sky and the earth. Only me.

"I love you, boy."

I take a few steps into the field, and it feels so good, so nice to be in the cool air, to smell the smells all around me. To feel the sun on my coat. I feel like I am here.

"You can go."

I gather my strength and I start off and it feels good, like I have no age at all, like I am timeless. I pick up speed. I run.

"It's okay, Enzo."

I don't look back, but I know he's there. I bark twice because I want him to hear, I want him to know. I feel his eyes on me, but I don't turn back. Off into the field, into the vastness of the universe ahead, I run.

"You can go," he calls to me.

Faster, the wind presses against my face as I run, faster, I feel my heart beating wildly and I bark twice to tell him, to tell everyone in the world, to say *faster!* I bark twice so he knows, so he remembers. What I want now is what I've always wanted.

One more lap, Denny! One more lap! *Faster!*

Imola, Italy

After it is all over, after the last race has been won, after the season's champion has been crowned, Denny sits alone in the infield of the Tamburello corner, on the grass that is soggy from many days of rain. A bright figure in his Ferrari-red racing suit. All around the world, people celebrate his victory. In the trailers and the back rooms, the other drivers, some of whom are half his age, shake their heads in amazement. To have accomplished what he has accomplished. To have endured what he has endured. To have become a Formula One champion out of nowhere. At his age. It is nothing less than a fairy tale.

An electric golf cart stops on the tarmac near him, driven by a young woman with long, golden hair. With her in the cart are two other figures, one large and one small.

The young woman climbs out and walks toward the champion.

"Dad?" she calls.

He looks to her, though he had hoped to be alone just a little longer.

"They're big fans," she says, indicating her passengers.

He smiles and rolls his eyes. The idea that he has fans at all—big or small—is very silly to him and something he has to get used to.

"No, no," she says, because she knows his thoughts almost before he can think them. "I think you'd really like to meet them."

He nods at her because she is always right. She beckons the two people in the cart. A man steps out, hunched beneath a rain poncho. Then a child. They walk toward the champion.

"*Dení!*" the man calls. "*Dení!* We hoped to find you here!"

"Here I am," the champion replies.

"Dení, we are your biggest fans. Your daughter brought us to find you. She said you would not mind."

"She knows me," the champion says warmly.

"My son," says the man. "He worships you. He talks about you always."

The champion looks at the boy, who is small with

sharp features and icy blue eyes and light, curly hair.

"How old are you?" he asks.

"Five," the boy replies.

"Do you race?"

"He races the karts," the father says. "He is very good. The first time he sat in a kart, he knew how to drive it. It's very expensive for me, but he is so good, such a talent, that we do it."

"Good," the champion says, "very good."

"Will you sign our program?" the father asks. "We watched the race from the field over there. The grandstand is very expensive. We drove from Napoli."

"Of course," the champion says to the father. He takes the program and the pen. "What's your name?" he asks the boy.

"*Enzo*," the boy says.

The champion looks up, startled. For a moment, he doesn't move. He doesn't write. He doesn't speak.

"Enzo?" he asks, finally.

"Yes," the boy says. "My name is Enzo. *Anch'io voglio diventare un campione.*"

Stunned, the champion stares at the boy.

"He says he wants to be a champion," the father translates, misinterpreting the pause. "Like you."

"Excellent idea," the champion says, but he continues

staring at the boy until he realizes he's been staring too long and shakes his head to stop himself. "Excuse me," he says. "Your son reminds me of a good friend of mine."

He catches his daughter's eye, then he signs the boy's program and hands it to the father, who reads it.

"What's this?" the father asks.

"My telephone number in Maranello," the champion says. "When you think your son is ready, call me. I'll make sure he gets proper instruction and the opportunity to drive."

"Thank you! Thank you very much!" the man says. "He talks about you always. He says you are the best champion ever. He says you are better, even, than Senna!"

The champion rises, his racing suit still wet from the rain. He pats the boy's head and ruffles his hair. The boy looks up at him.

"He is a race car driver at heart," the champion says.

"Thank you," the father says. "He studies all of your races on videotapes."

"*La macchina va dove vanno gli occhi*," the boy says.

The champion laughs, then looks to the sky.

"Yes," he says. "The car goes where the eyes go. It is true, my young friend. It is very, very true."

Acknowledgments

Thanks to the wonderful people at Harper Children's, especially Alyson Day and Phoebe Ych; Jeff Kleinman and my fantastic team at Folio Literary Management; my resident experts and facilitators, including but not limited to Scott Driscoll, Jasen Emmons, Joe Fugere, Bob Harrison, Soyon Im, Doug Katz, David Katzenberg, Don Kitch Jr., Michael Lord, Layne Mayheu, Kevin O'Brien, Nick O'Connell, Luigi Orsenigo, Sandy and Steve Perlbinder, Jenn Risko, Bob Rogers, Paula Schaap, Jennie Shortridge, Marvin and Landa Stein, Dawn Stuart, Terry Tirrell, Brian Towey, Cassidy Turner, Andrea Vitalich, Kevin York, Lawrence Zola . . .

Caleb, Eamon, and Dashiell . . .

and the one who makes my world possible, Drella.

RACING
in the RAIN
MY LIFE AS A DOG

Read an interview with author Garth Stein

Check out cool photos of Garth racing, his dog, Comet, and more!

Q&A WITH GARTH STEIN:

Q: Where did the idea for the book come from?
A: The first seed for this book was planted in my mind about ten years ago. I was no longer working in documentary films, but a friend asked me to help with the U.S. distribution of a film he knew about from Mongolia called *State of Dogs*. I didn't end up getting involved with the film, but the idea really stuck with me. In Mongolia, there is a belief that the next life for a dog is as a man. I thought this was a cool concept and I tucked it away, thinking I might someday do something with it.

Q: What challenges did you face as you were writing from a dog's point of view?
A: Enzo, as a dog, has certain limitations: he has no thumbs, for instance; he has a long, floppy tongue that can't be used to form words. But Enzo, as a dog, also has certain advantages: people will say things in front him because it is assumed he doesn't understand. People will allow him to see some things for the same reason—Enzo is a fly on the wall. I had a great deal of fun playing with this idea.

Q: Is there any significance to the name Enzo?
A: Yes! Denny's dog, Enzo, is named after Enzo Ferrari, who built one of the greatest car trademarks in the world. Ferrari automobiles are famous everywhere. And Ferrari is a serious player in the world of Formula 1 racing.

But I have a funny story about how I arrived at Enzo's name. . . .

When I first started writing this novel, Enzo was not named Enzo. He was named Juan Pablo, after Juan Pablo Montoya, the race car driver. When my wife read the first few pages, she said that she loved what I was writing, but the name of the dog wasn't quite right.

"How about Enzo?" she asked. We had two sons already, and were expecting our third. I had always wanted to name one of my boys Enzo. I thought it was the ultimate cool name: Enzo Stein. But my wife very much disagreed. "We have a lot of different nationalities in our combined backgrounds," she reasoned. "Russian, German, Austrian, Tlingit Indian, Irish, English . . . but we have no Italian."

"But then we won't be able to name the baby Enzo," I said.

"I thought of that," she said, nodding slowly.

"I really wanted to name him Enzo," I said.

"Enzo, the dog, is your new baby," she replied. "And when our new baby comes, we'll find the right name for him."

(For those of you who are interested: We named our son Dashiell.)

Q: Are you a dog owner yourself? Who is *your* Enzo?
A: Yes, I have a dog named Comet, who is a Lab/poodle mix. But she's no Enzo. She's a little too silly and sweet. Let me put it to you this way: she has a few more lifetimes to live as a dog before she's ready to return as a person. Unless you could guarantee that she could come back as a ball girl at Wimbledon. She's awesome with a tennis ball!

Q: There are some very sad moments in the book, as Denny loses his wife and then his daughter. How did those difficult events contribute to Denny's development as a character? How did they contribute to Enzo?
A: A character is tested when he or she is truly pushed to the

4

brink. The way the story is set up, we know that it is not about Denny trying his hardest and then accepting defeat. This is a story that will test Denny's inner strength. Because of their relationship, it is only appropriate that, at some point, Denny must rely on his greatest ally, Enzo, given the feelings that they have for each other.

Q: Enzo's lap around the track at Thunderhill Raceway Park with Denny is definitely one of the most joyous and truthful passages we have ever read. The beauty of life is really captured in that last turn around the track. What was your inspiration for that scene?

A: When I wrote that scene, I was totally engaged in the writing process. I knew I had to get Enzo into a race car, and then I let him do the writing. You know, having raced cars myself, I will say that, when screaming down a straight and flying through some turns, even the most serious person is little more than a happy dog, his head out the window, hoping for the moment to last a little longer.

Q: Can you elaborate on the art of racing in the rain? Is it the ability to anticipate the next move or the ability to trust oneself to make the next move without anticipation?

A: Well, yes and yes. It's also about letting go of self-doubt and insecurity. Once a good rain racer commits to a decision, he follows it to completion because he knows that certain things must play out. If we are acting entirely with our best interests in mind—not the best interests of our ego, but the best interests of our soul—we are acting properly.

I have to refer back to the epigraph: "With your mind power, your determination, your instinct, and the experience as well, you can fly very high." That was said by Aryton Senna, who was arguably the best rain racer ever. I think he's talking about this idea: there is no limit to what we can accomplish if we believe in ourselves completely.

Q: THE ART OF RACING IN THE RAIN is dedicated to your childhood dog, Muggs. I know you have told the story of the Muggs dedication and your father's reaction to it before, but could I ask you to tell it one more time here? It's a wonderful story.
A: My family's childhood dog was an Airedale named Muggs. She was a sweet, lovable, proud dog. And she got old. When I was a teenager, one day my father came home from work early. He was wearing his suit, and it seemed odd to see him in the day at home in a suit. He put Muggs in the car and took her away. He came back without her. (She was quite old, her hips had given way, and she wasn't doing well. . . .)

When he came back, he took all of her things out of the place we kept them in her cabinet. Her bowls, her food, her leashes, her collar. He put them in a garbage bag, tied it up, and placed it outside by the garbage cans. That was it. He never said a word about it, and no one in our house spoke of it.

When I finished my book, I wanted to dedicate it to someone, but I didn't know who. So I dedicated it to Muggs, knowing that I was really dedicating it to my father by doing that.

The book was ready, I got my first copy from HarperCollins, and I proudly showed my parents, forgetting for a moment that I had dedicated it to Muggs. My father opened the book, saw the dedication page . . . and started crying.

So he knew. Parents know stuff like that. He knew I meant it was for him.

Check out cool photos of Garth racing, his dog, Comet, and more!

Garth and his dog, Comet, at the beach

Comet relaxing at home

Garth's studio

Garth and Comet at New Year's

At the Mazda MX-5 Cup with a new fan

Garth and Comet playing around

Garth at a reading

With friend and producer Johan Lindgren and Comet